WHODUNIT ANTIQUES

BOOK 2: A STAB IN THE DARK

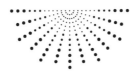

SHELLY WEST

By Shelly West

CHAPTER ONE

Abigail struggled to breathe in enough air while she chased after Thor, her Great Dane. He wasn't poorly leash-trained by any means, but the difficulty of keeping up with him came down to simple math: One of his strides amounted to five of Abigail's.

"Thor," she gasped. "Thor, wait up!"

The Great Dane heard her sputtering call, immediately made an abrupt U-Turn in the middle of the empty sidewalk, and came bounding back toward her. His long legs covered the considerable distance between them in just a few seconds.

Abigail wheezed as Thor licked her hand encouragingly. She had decided she'd never miss a morning walk after moving down to Wallace Point and seeing how nice and quiet it was. Now she doubted her decision.

Thor, of course, was a huge proponent of the walks. Living in a cramped city apartment for years could do that to a dog.

Abigail's lungs burned despite the good breeze, and she felt a serious cramp starting in her side. "That's it," she huffed, slowing from her tortured jog to a more comfortable walk. "No more."

Thor bowed his head, then slowly looked up at her in disappointment.

"Oh, don't take that tone of face with me," Abigail warned, wagging a finger in front of his large nose. "We weren't all built for galloping like you."

Thor sneezed at the compliment, as if to say, "I suppose I won't hold it against you."

Abigail knew the neighborhood better now than she had a few weeks ago and soon they were walking up to Grandma's antique store, Whodunit Antiques. The store wouldn't open for a couple of hours, but the sheriff's car was already parked in the customer lot.

"Look, Thor," Abigail said. "Sheriff Wilson caught Grandma bright and early today, didn't he?"

Thor trotted to the driver's door and sniffed it. He looked back at Abigail, shot her a reassuring grin, jerked his leash from her hands and leaped onto the front porch, where he collapsed into a big, satisfied heap. Abigail shook her head as she walked up the steps, unclipping his leash before she headed in.

The front door was unlocked, as usual. Grandma refused

to lock her doors, even after the store had been broken into during one of the most exciting murder cases Wallace Point had seen in years.

The case started with someone breaking into Grandma's store in search of an antique. Grandma, alerted by her Shih Tzu Missy's whimpering, had come down the stairs in the middle of the night to find the source of the noise. She got more than she had bargained for when she tripped over a dead body.

The fall had landed Grandma in the hospital, which was the only reason Abigail discovered she had another living family member besides her mother, Sarah. Abigail sighed. Her mom wasn't exactly forthcoming when it came to her past.

Sheriff Wilson and Grandma sat at the kitchen table with cups of steaming coffee in front of them and a heaping plate of cookies between them.

"Good morning, Grandma, Sheriff Wilson," Abigail said. She walked to the sink and poured herself a glass of water. Missy greeted Abigail with a quick trot around her ankles and then settled again underneath Grandma's feet.

As soon as Abigail took her first sip of water, she knew that something wasn't right. The room was too quiet, as if Grandma and the Sheriff had stopped talking just before she entered.

"Good morning, dear," Grandma finally said, her eyes still on the sheriff. "How was your run?"

"Awful. But at least Thor enjoyed it." Abigail washed out

her glass and placed it on the drying rack. "Shame on you, Sheriff Wilson, for pulling my sweet Grandma out of bed so early."

Sheriff Wilson glanced up at her. His eyes looked puffy and tired, and it took him a moment to understand she had spoken to him. "Eh? What was that, Abigail?"

Yup, something was definitely up. Grandma usually had Sheriff Wilson's full attention. In fact, Grandma usually had the full attention of most older men. Today, however, Sheriff Wilson was obviously preoccupied.

"Sweetheart," Grandma cut in, "I feel like pancakes this morning. Why don't you take a shower while I whip some up?"

Abigail paused. What was Grandma up to? Was she just trying to get Abigail out of the room? But Abigail only nodded. "Pancakes sound great, Grandma. Just give me thirty minutes."

ABIGAIL DIDN'T ACTUALLY NEED thirty minutes, but she wanted to give Sheriff Wilson plenty of time with Grandma.

When she walked back into the kitchen, the sheriff was gone and in his place at the table was a plate full of steaming pancakes. Bits of chocolate formed smiley faces on each pancake. Some faces had freckles.

"So, what's going on with the sheriff?"

Grandma flipped a final pancake onto her plate and eased into a chair. "He's got skeletons falling out of his closets."

"What?"

"Just the past refusing to stay in the past. You know that stabbing at the motel?"

"The one that happened right when I moved in? Yeah, how could I forget?"

"Well, the newspaper had suggested it could be an infamous serial killer."

"Suggested is an understatement." Abigail finished smothering her pancakes with butter and real maple syrup. "I can still remember that headline. *Wallace Point Ripper Stabs Again!* For a small town newspaper, they do love their gore."

"Yes. It was rather sensational of them. Anyway, Willy has the Ripper on his mind."

"But I thought it wasn't really the Ripper. Something to do with out-of-towners, right?"

Grandma nodded. "The more details that came out, the less likely it seemed to be our local serial stabber. But it still has brought up some bad memories for Willy. He has a complicated history with the Ripper, you see."

"I didn't know that."

"He doesn't talk about it much. It was a tough time for him. You might not believe it now, but Willy was a talented detective. He was on his way up. Nothing could stump him." Grandma looked off, possibly remembering a younger, brighter Willy Wilson. "But then the Wallace Point Ripper came along, and Willy couldn't solve the case. He followed every lead, pursued every angle. Nothing. Since then, he hasn't been the same. He lost his confidence, his spark. I guess you could say it broke him."

"Wow. That's awful."

"It is. Ever since, he hasn't been comfortable with any case that isn't open and shut. And now the big fuss at the motel has brought it all back for him." Grandma refilled her cup of coffee and, without meeting Abigail's gaze, added, "I wouldn't bring it up around him, dear, if you can avoid it."

That was a surprise.

It made sense that Willy wouldn't want to discuss the Ripper. But it seemed odd that Grandma felt the need to warn Abigail away from future conversations. In a town where rumors spread like wildfire, and where everyone else already knew all the details, why the extra caution? Abigail took another bite of her pancakes. "Sure, Grandma. The story is safe with me."

IT WAS a quiet morning for the store—too quiet for Grandma's taste.

"Something's up," she said from her seat behind the checkout counter, her eyes peering sharply into the vacant parking lot. "I'm going to fix a plate of cookies and take them… take them… Well, I'll take them somewhere and find out exactly what's going on."

"You always do, Grandma," Abigail said, pausing from her

work researching a colorful Tiffany lamp Grandma had recently acquired at an auction. "We can take my car if you like."

"No, thank you, dear. I wouldn't want to trouble you. Willy probably just lost his cat up a tree again. Last time that happened, he shut down the entire town. And during tourist season too."

"That must be some cat."

"It's twenty-five years old. Going for a world record, I think. Anyhow, I'm going to close for lunch and meet up with the gals."

"Gals?"

Grandma smirked. "You've met them before. I heard that you apparently call them the 'Granny Gang.'"

"Oh, *those* gals. Yeah, well, I had quite the first encounter with them."

"When was this?"

"When you were in the hospital. They arrived at the store in a bunch of golf carts and swarmed the place. It felt like a police raid!"

"How silly. They're just a bunch of old harmless coots. We like to exchange gossip while we sew us up some sock monkeys. Nothing more."

"Sock monkeys? I thought recently you told me you couldn't sew."

Grandma's expression grew dire. "That's right. I can't. My sock monkeys tend to be... How do I put it kindly? Sock monstrosities. I usually end up having to burn them in fear they might come to life and take revenge on their creator."

"Now I kinda want to see one of these things."

"Trust me; you don't. And anyhow, I'm not there for the sock monkeys. I'm there for the gossip."

"Then gossip away, Grandma, and let me know what you find out. Meanwhile, I think I'll pay Sally a visit."

"Sounds like a plan… And sounds like we'll be pretty busy today. Is Friday Movie Night still on?"

Abigail smiled. "You know I'd never miss it."

Grandma reached out to Abigail for a hug, which Abigail returned. "Just think, two months ago I had never met my granddaughter. Now I get to see her every day."

THE WALK to the Book Cafe, Sally's coffee shop and rare books store, was short and pleasant. Summer was giving way to autumn, with the first whispers of cool weather kissing the air.

Abigail stepped into the cafe, the tiny bell above the door announcing her entrance. The little shop smelled of fresh coffee and the innermost pages of old books. Sunlight poured in through the large glass windows, tinting everything gold and brown.

Sally stood at the counter, facing away as she spoke excitedly into her phone. Not that there were many customers at the moment. In fact, Abigail was the only one.

Sally Kent made the best coffee Abigail had ever tasted, and so the Book Cafe was rarely vacant, even during the quiet season. Yet here Abigail was, the only customer. Maybe Grandma was right that something was up today.

Abigail, not wanting to interrupt, sought out the book she had been reading from the bookshelf. The Book Cafe acted like an unofficial library of antique books. The books had to stay at the cafe, but customers could read as many as they wanted.

Abigail found her current book, one on steamships from the early 1900s. A blue sloth bookmarker marked her place, and she began reading about the SS Atlantic. This ship was quite a bit larger than the schooner she had saved from pirates during her first visit to Wallace Point.

Abigail paused to shake her head incredulously. Sometimes even *she* didn't believe she had managed to do that.

Sally hung up the phone and whipped around, her blonde ponytail flying out over her shoulders. Her face, usually bright and perky, positively glowed with the excitement of fresh gossip. "Oh, Abigail! Have you heard?"

Abigail closed the book and put it away, suspecting she wasn't going to get any more reading done. "No. What's the buzz?"

"James Wilson is back in town!"

"Who?"

"Sheriff Wilson's son! He just arrived, and after all these years, he's here to help his father with the big case."

"The investigation into the stabbing? I thought that was over."

Sally shrugged, a happy bounce to her shoulders. "I guess not! Now, you know what this means, don't you?"

"No. What does it mean?"

"Fresh meat! You're off the hook as the newbie in town."

Abigail frowned, taking in this new information. The Sheriff's son... If he had been gone all this time, why would he come back now? It wasn't like this stabbing was that big of a case, especially compared to what happened with the ship earlier.

A distant honking pervaded the store, shaking Abigail out of her thoughts. The symphony of horns grew closer and louder, until finally a fleet of old ladies in tricked out golf carts came into view through the big store windows.

Sally whispered in awe, "The Granny Gang. There's thousands of them!"

Abigail stood, getting a closer look. "I would say about a couple of dozen at best."

"Still, you never see them all together like this unless something big is going down."

Abigail squinted, trying to make out the golf cart taking the lead. "Grandma?" she said in realization, but the horde of golf carts peeled away before she could think to go out and greet them.

Sally commented, "Dang, they're on a mission, huh?"

Abigail shook her head in disbelief. "Whatever she's up to, Grandma better not get into too much trouble!"

CHAPTER TWO

Abigail pressed the lid tight over the large saucepan. Inside, yellow corn kernels were just starting to explode into white puffs. Here and there came a little *pop!* Keeping the lid closed tight, she swirled the saucepan over the hot stove, spreading heat into all of the nooks and crannies.

Pop! Pop! Popopopopopopop!

When the tiny explosions slowed down, Abigail pulled the pan off the heat. She dumped the popcorn into a large ceramic bowl and drizzled salt and melted butter on top. She mixed it all together with a wooden spoon, then carried the bowl with her into the small living room.

Thor was already stretched out in front of the couch, with Missy sitting in Grandma's chair. The ancient TV and

VCR Abigail had discovered in the attic were set up on an end table. The VHS tape Grandma had picked out sat on an old cardboard box on top of the television with the remote. They had already tested all three pieces of antiquated technology and learned that, miraculously, everything still worked. Since then, for the past couple of weeks, Friday had officially been dubbed Movie Night.

Everything was all set. Now all that was missing was Grandma.

Right on cue, the sound of a golf cart's musical horn sent Missy flying out of her chair and hurtling toward the front door. Her cream and gold body turned into a tiny sphere of fur and irrepressible excitement.

Thor didn't bother to get up. He knew the tune pretty well by now and wasn't concerned. He did, however, have the decency to thump his tail against the floor when Grandma waltzed in with Missy in her arms.

"Why, hello, Grandma," Abigail said from the couch. She tossed a popped kernel into the air and caught it in her mouth. "Fancy seeing you here at our store."

Grandma flopped onto the couch as floppily as a little white-haired lady could flop. "Don't be sore with me, dear. I bet you didn't have a customer all afternoon."

"I'm not sore. I did miss you, though. But you're right. Not a single customer."

"Murders are bad for business."

"So is fresh meat."

"Oh, I would hardly call James fresh meat. He is more of a prodigal son."

Abigail leaned forward. She surmised that Grandma had just spent all afternoon with her senior citizen cohorts grilling James Wilson. Maybe Grandma had picked up something interesting. "So, what juicy details did you dig up?"

"Well, James's business is booming, but he's taking some time off to help his father."

"Sally mentioned he wants to pitch in with the stabbing case. What exactly does James do?"

"He's a private investigator. Takes after his father, in a way."

"Grandma, don't you think it's kind of odd for James to show up now?"

"What do you mean?"

"Why not show up for Reginald's murder? That was big news. This stabbing case seems just about closed."

Grandma grabbed a small handful of popcorn. "Apparently it isn't. I guess Wallace Point lost interest when we realized it wasn't the Ripper, but the real killer still hasn't been found." She got up from the couch, leaving Missy to keep her seat warm. "Don't worry about James. I watched that boy grow into a man in this town. And such a handsome man too. Anyhow, let's start this wonderful picture. You're going to love it!"

Grandma did manage to start the movie, but she nodded off on Abigail's shoulder before the end of the opening credits. Abigail watched the whole thing. She didn't quite love it on account of the movie's slow pace, but she did get a kick out of rewinding the tape.

The next morning, Abigail was still thinking about James Wilson's sudden appearance as she started out on her run with Thor. After a few agonized steps, she decided the run would be more of a walk.

Walking gave her more time to take a look around her. The sun was rising later these days, and the sky was more gray than blue. Birds called to each other from tree to tree, creating a terrible racket that Abigail was gradually coming to appreciate.

She took a deep breath of the crisp morning air, then relaxed her body to allow her mind to muse over James's sudden arrival. Grandma didn't seem to see anything amiss about James Wilson's timing, and, to be honest, Abigail couldn't come up with a solid reason to be suspicious. And yet she was.

If James's own business was booming, why drop everything to come back to work on a random small town crime? Why hadn't he showed up when Reginald Grimes's body washed up on shore? That had been a big case, perhaps bigger than this motel stabbing.

Then again, if the recent stabbing wasn't a big deal, why hadn't it been closed yet? A month without an arrest seemed like a long time for a murder case.

Abigail groaned. She had lots of questions, but no answers.

Just then, Abigail spotted an unusually large hat in a garden full of unusually large vegetables. The hat hid the face, neck, and shoulders of whoever was wearing it. All Abigail could see was a hint of a pink dress amidst the immense foliage.

Beneath the hat, a woman's voice cooed, "There you go, sweet thing, that's it. Unfurl those lovely leaves. Show the other gourds who's the boss."

Abigail paused at the garden gate. An archway curved over the gate, and it was covered in enormous yellow roses. Their scent was sweet and strong.

The voice under the hat continued, "Now what is this pesky thing doing here? We'll just *yank* that right out, won't we? There. Better? Lovely roses, aren't they?"

It took Abigail a second to realize that last sentence was meant for her. "Uh, yeah. Sorry, I didn't mean to sneak up on you."

The hat picked itself up off the ground and unfolded into a willowy woman. Her pink dress reached her knees, and both knees and garment were stained with dirt. "You didn't sneak up on me. If anything, I sneaked up on you. You seemed pretty lost in thought."

"I was trying to come up with answers to questions I don't have yet."

"Ah, that makes you the second person this morning."

Abigail froze. "Who was the first?"

"James. Nice surprise. I hadn't seen him since graduation. Speaking of losing oneself, you seem to know your way around better than that one time you got lost."

Abigail was still trying to absorb the tidbit about James. "How do you know about that?"

"Well, you hobbled past my garden about five times."

"Oh. I guess that makes sense."

"I'm always out here early to chat with my plants, and I saw you huffing and puffing. I've seen enough runners to know what a newbie looks like."

"Ah. Well, I'm Abigail. Nice to meet you."

"I'm Camille. Camille Bellerose. You're Granny Lane's granddaughter, right?"

"Yes." Abigail studied the woman. She looked a few years older than Abigail. Her face was open and seemed honest, and she met Abigail's gaze steadily. She looked like a no-nonsense individual, like a teacher a kid would both like and respect. "It's nice to meet you, Camille. You have a beautiful garden. Everything is so... big."

For the first time, Camille's face broke into a grin. "Thank you! My pumpkins have beaten world records." Camille looked up and down the empty street, as if scouting for spies. "Want to know the secret?"

"Uh, sure."

"You have to keep them company. They hate being alone all the time. Plants are quite extroverted, you see."

Okay. This woman was either crazy or pulling Abigail's leg. She had to be. But the longer Abigail stared at Camille, the more she felt convinced Camille wasn't crazy or joking, but perfectly serious.

"Yep, that's me. Child wrangler by day, gardener extraordinaire by dawn."

"Child wrangler?"

"I teach at the elementary school. Not surprised at all, are you? No one ever is. In high school, I was voted most likely to become a teacher. Now, you know what I tell my kids when they can't figure out answers to questions they don't have?"

Abigail perked up. "What's that?"

"Go to the library."

It was another slow day for the store, so Grandma encouraged Abigail to take the afternoon off. It was such a beautiful day outside that Abigail couldn't say no. Besides, she knew exactly where she wanted to go.

The Wallace Point Public Library was breathtaking. The vaulted ceilings were beautifully painted with scenes from ancient fairytales. The rooms had shelves of books stacked to the ceilings, with sliding ladders positioned everywhere to help patrons reach the top. Rows of tables were lined with lamps for studying. The place was so unexpectedly immense that Abigail didn't know where to start.

She decided to begin with the librarian.

The woman's wrinkled skin hung off her bony frame. A

neat bun pulled her salt and pepper hair tightly away from her long face. She peered at Abigail over her perfectly round glasses. "Let me get this straight. You're looking for answers to questions you don't have yet."

Abigail wondered for a moment if this librarian was a psychic. "Exactly. How did you know?"

"You're at a library."

"Oh. Well, I guess I'm thinking there's something up with the stabbings that happened at the motel a month ago."

"Aha! Lucky you, we have an archive of every local newspaper printing, going all the way back to the 1800s. But as for this motel murder, I only recall it being covered in a few recent reports written in the Wallace Point Beacon."

Abigail shook her head. "I think I read those when they came out."

"Try an online search. Other towns may have printed their own version of events. Follow me." The librarian escorted Abigail to a boxy old computer, where she pulled up a database. "Enter your search terms here, and you should find what you're looking for."

Abigail took a seat and watched the librarian return to the front desk. Abigail knew her phone's internet browser was probably faster than this old machine, but she felt it'd be a bit rude and awkward to pull it out now, after the librarian seemed so pleased with herself.

She sighed and typed in the appropriate search terms. Many nearby towns had picked up the story, but none of them had done any investigative journalism. The articles only repeated what Abigail had originally read in The Wallace Point Beacon.

This investigation wasn't turning out to be very productive... Then Abigail thought of something.

She punched into the old computer the search term: *James Wilson Private Investigator.*

She had to scroll all the way down the results page before she found a link to his website. Abigail snorted. The page was simple and dated. It advertised services such as *Spousal Surveillance* and *Background Checks*. Every page had a tacky animated image of a dog detective holding a magnifying glass while he followed some obvious footprints.

If business was booming, James certainly wasn't investing any of it into his online presence.

Crummy website, yes, but did it mean James was up to something? Not really. Reluctantly, Abigail decided to call it a day and head home for dinner with Grandma.

Just as she was about to walk out of the grand double doors, the librarian caught up with her. "Young lady, this just arrived at my front desk."

"What is it?"

"Today's newspaper." She pressed the roll of pages into Abigail's hands.

One headline jumped out at her as she unfolded the paper: *Reporter Apologizes for Sensationalizing Motel Murder.*

"Keep it," the librarian said, smiling triumphantly for helping a patron in need. "That was my personal copy anyway."

"Thanks!" Abigail started to flip to the story when a thought popped into her head. "Has anyone else come in today asking about the murders?"

The librarian paused at the door. "Yes, actually. Dear old James. I hadn't seen that child in years!"

CHAPTER THREE

"Something wrong with the meatloaf, honey?" Grandma asked from across the table. Abigail looked up, realizing she hadn't said a word to her grandmother for minutes, instead pushing her meal around her plate.

"No, Grandma. This meatloaf is the best I ever had."

She wasn't kidding. She had always thought meatloaf was gray, bland, and boring. This meatloaf wasn't the case by a long shot. It was juicy and savory yet somehow lightly sweet. Just taking a bite made Abigail happier.

"You seem lost in your thoughts."

"Apparently that's me today."

"What's on your mind?"

"That reporter who covered the motel stabbings. Did you know she issued an apology?"

"Why, that's old news." Grandma grinned wickedly, and

Abigail was once again reminded never to underestimate her grandmother.

"Do you know more than today's paper?"

"Of course."

"Grandma, spill the beans!"

"The newspaper said the reporter admitted to sensationalizing her story on purpose. The newspaper also said the reporter issued a public apology for this."

"Right."

Grandma delicately dabbed a napkin against her lips. "Well, what the newspaper didn't say was why. The reporter claims she did it to help the newspaper itself. Reginald's murder, the theft of the Lafayette, and all those stories caused a significant boost in sales. She wanted to keep that going."

Abigail leaned back in her chair. "You don't seem convinced."

"I never knew Rachel Cuthbert to be so selfless."

"Wait, you know the reporter?"

"Yes. Rachel grew up here. You know how small Wallace Point is, and how old I am, so of course I've had my run-ins with her. Oh, and I should probably mention that she was a friend of your mother's as well."

Somehow Abigail wasn't surprised. A disgraced journalist did seem like the type of person her mother would have associated with. "But you think Rachel didn't mean to sensationalize those stories?"

"No, I believe she did. What I don't believe is that she did it to help the newspaper. And there's something else the paper didn't report: She's on hiatus."

"Is that important?"

"It could be, because it wasn't her choice. The paper forced her to take leave. That makes me wonder just how sorry she really is if she's on hiatus involuntarily."

"How do you know all this? Did the Granny Gang tell you?"

"You know, Abigail, they are just tickled to death that you nicknamed them that. A couple of them are talking about getting leather vests and tattoos. But no, it wasn't the Granny Gang who told me. James came by today."

Abigail just about choked. She had been everywhere James Wilson had gone today, yet she still hadn't managed to catch up to him.

"Honey, are you all right? I don't think the girls are entirely serious about getting tattoos. Although, I wouldn't put it past a few of them."

"No, Grandma, it's not that. I mean, tattoos at their age would be pretty funny, but I'm surprised James came by. It seems we keep just missing each other."

"James was always good about keeping up with his neighbors. He's probably popping in on everyone, and I wouldn't be surprised if he kept visiting people right up until he left to return to the city. Though who knows when that will be."

Abigail decided to forget James for now. She had a more suspicious person of interest she wanted to speak to. "Grandma, do you know where I can find Rachel Cuthbert?"

"Last I knew she was living in an apartment above Kirby's Candlepin Alley."

"That must be a noisy place to live above."

Grandma interlaced her fingers. "Sure, but I get the feeling that, for Rachel, home is just a place to crash for the night. Now, finish up your meatloaf. I made apple pie."

PIPER FISCHER WAS a welcome distraction during yet another quiet morning at the store. Her fiery hair floated in soft curls around her face, and her wide eyes sparkled with excitement. She greeted them with her usual, "How are you two lovely ladies today?"

"We're great," Grandma responded, setting down her ledger. "But you seem even better. What's got you so excited?"

"I just saw James! It's so good to see him again. The town feels complete with him here."

Grandma grinned. "I noticed. The whole town can't talk about much else. Well, besides the murder. But I'm afraid we're making Abigail feel neglected now that she's not the main focus of the town gossip."

Abigail froze as the two looked at her. "Not at all," she finally said. "I'm just wondering why he came here to help with this case but not with the murder of Reginald."

"Well, this case is quite different," Piper began as she picked up one of Grandma's cookies. "It has brought back the name of the Ripper, who Sheriff Wilson has quite a terrible history with." She stopped to look over at Grandma. "She knows about what happened, right?"

Grandma shook her head. "I told her a little bit, but... Oh, it's such an awful situation." She looked away.

Piper chose not to elaborate, for Grandma's sake. "Anyway, I think it's sweet of James to visit, at least to give poor Willy some moral support."

Abigail paused, reevaluating her initial suspicions about James. "Yeah," she finally admitted. "Grandma told me about how the Ripper got away with several murders, so I can see how Sheriff Wilson feels partially responsible. I guess I hadn't thought about that." She changed the subject. "So Piper, do you know Rachel Cuthbert?"

"The reporter? Enough to say hello."

"Do you happen to know where she likes to hang out after work?"

"No, sorry. She and I don't really keep up."

Yet another dead lead. Abigail waved it off. "That's okay. Grandma, mind if I duck out? I'm having that coffee party with Sally today."

Piper tilted her head. "Isn't every day a coffee party at Sally's cafe?"

Grandma took a bite of a cookie. "Actually this is a very special coffee party. More like a tea party, with all the fancy sandwiches and cookies. Go ahead, dear. I'll keep Piper company while she picks out what she wants to buy." Piper looked like she was about to protest, but Grandma cut her off. "Now, Piper, you know the rules. One cookie means one purchase."

Abigail grinned as she made her way out of the store and into the late morning sunshine. Grandma knew that Piper, heiress of the Fischer whaling family estate and lover of fine antiquities, could afford a trinket or two.

THE SIGN in Sally Kent's cafe window said "Closed" but Abigail walked right in. Sally had discovered a few rare books on the fine art of hosting proper tea parties and she had asked Abigail to be her guinea pig. They wouldn't be having tea, of course.

Abigail wasn't about to complain. Sally made the finest coffee Abigail had ever tasted. If she had to choose one word to describe it, the word was *divine.*

Sally bounced toward her. She had curled her blond hair so her ponytail tumbled in glossy locks over her shoulders, and she wore a pastel blue dress that fell to her calves. Abigail suddenly felt underdressed in her jeans and top, but Sally didn't seem to mind. "Abigail!" she squeaked. "What do you think?"

Gentle piano music played in the background. One of the customer tables was draped with a white tablecloth and set with fine china, cloth napkins, teacups, tiny spoons, sugar cubes, and on and on. In the center of the table, a three-tiered tower displayed finger sandwiches, cuts of fruits, and bite-sized desserts.

It all looked quite pretty, not to mention delicious. Abigail's stomach growled. If she had known how elaborate this coffee party was going to be, she would have volunteered to help.

"It looks great, Sally. I can't believe you did all this!"

"I know." Sally giggled. "It's a bit much. But you should read these books. Tea time has such a rich tradition. And all those rules about what goes where evolved from trying to make everyone as comfortable as possible. Then I got to thinking how coffee doesn't really have a tradition like that, and I thought why not have a coffee party? I got so excited, I went all out!"

Abigail laughed. "Well, thanks for inviting me. Show me everything."

The little bell above the door jingled and Bobby Kent, Sally's dad, made his usual grand entrance. Bobby had once hosted a popular game show in California. Now he hosted "Bobby's Big Bingo" on Saturday nights in Wallace Point. It was a smaller gig, but he hadn't lost his flair.

Today, he wore a rust-colored one piece jumpsuit, with an oversized zipper that ran all the way down the front. He flashed them a huge smile and gave them his trademark double finger-guns point. "How's my little girl?"

"Your little girl is throwing a coffee party. How's it look?"

"Well, honey, I think it looks lovely," Bobby said, his voice undulating as if he were announcing a huge prize. "Am I invited?"

"Not this time. Ladies only. You know, the whole girls rule, boys drool thing. But don't worry. Next time, you and I will have a coffee party all to ourselves. Then I'll debut my new little tradition to the public."

"Sure thing, sweetheart. I'll get out of your way!"

"Wait!" Abigail said before Bobby Kent could make his grand exit. "Quick question. Do either of you know Rachel Cuthbert?"

"The reporter? Sure, we both know who she is." Sally said, obviously confused.

"Do either of you know where I can find her? I mean, I know where she lives, but I'd like to, let's say, 'accidentally' run into her so we can have a candid chat."

Sally shook her head, but Bobby nodded thoughtfully. "She lives right above Kirby's Candlepin Alley, and considering that Kirby serves beer, I wouldn't be surprised to find her there."

Abigail had already known Rachel lived above the bowling alley, but she hadn't thought to check the bar itself. Abigail stood. "Thank you, Bobby. I think that's a great place to start."

Bobby shot her with two more finger guns. "Hey, hey! Anytime, kiddo, anytime!"

After he left, Sally took a moment to study Abigail. "What are you up to? You have a mischievous air about you, just like you did when you were investigating Reginald's murder."

"I'll tell you all about it later, but first you need to show me which cup I'm supposed to drink coffee out of." Abigail moved to a chair and sat down as gracefully as she could. Before her was an array of cups, plates, and saucers, and she had no idea where to start.

Sally was silent for a moment, before admitting, "I don't know either. How do traditions get started? Are they just made up as they go along?"

Abigail shrugged and smiled. "Let's start making up some traditions then."

CHAPTER FOUR

After Abigail helped Sally come up with a rather elaborate coffee party tradition, she returned to the store to find Grandma in the parking lot turning on the golf cart.

"No time to explain!" Grandma said as she threw the register keys at Abigail. "Can you cover the store for a bit?"

"Yeah, of course. Somebody fall down a well or something?"

"No, Miss Eleanor's poodle ripped up her sock monkey stash and now we're way behind on our stock for tourist season! We're getting together for an emergency sock monkey sewing session, before it's too late."

"Sounds serious. Go on then. I've got things covered here."

Grandma saluted and peeled out of the parking lot, pushing her pink bedazzled golf cart to its limit.

Abigail knew the old ladies sold sock monkeys, but apparently she never knew what a big hustle it was. Though Abigail had yet to experience a tourist season, Grandma had told her tales of sock monkey exploits. According to her, the Granny Gang would roam the crowded streets on their golf carts, enticing children with their eclectic wares and guilt-tripping parents to cough up the money to buy them.

ABIGAIL WORKED the register for a couple of hours until Grandma finally returned, looking happy but exhausted. "How was it?" she asked.

Grandma had something tucked under her sweater. "It was fine."

"What are you hiding there, Grandma?"

Grandma pretended to be confused. "What are you talking about?"

"That thing tucked under your arm."

"Oh, that? I, um… I need to go out to the backyard for a moment, to burn it."

"Oh. One of your sock monstrosities? Why do the gals let you make them in the first place if you always have to destroy them after?"

"They think I'll get better at it one day, but they really ought to ask themselves… at what cost? At what cost?"

"Okay, well burn it quickly, because I've got a suspect to interview this evening."

Grandma nodded and hurried off to the backyard with a match in hand.

AT DUSK, Abigail prepared to head out for the bowling alley. It was a nice night for a walk. Ripper or no Ripper on the loose, Abigail was going to enjoy the evening as much as Grandma had enjoyed her afternoon.

There was a hint of a chill in the air, so Abigail grabbed her favorite scarf before heading out. The scarf was extra long and extra fluffy, and since it was charcoal gray, it went with just about everything in her closet. She wound it around her neck and stepped out into the cool evening, telling Thor, "You guard the house now, okay?"

He gave a low ruff and stationed himself next to the door.

The sun was just setting, painting the sky pink with shades of blue. The street lamps blinked on as she walked, their light filtering through the leaves of the grand old oaks that graced the wide sidewalks. It was the most comfortable feeling, letting the cool ocean breeze pinch her face while she burrowed her chin into her scarf.

The candlepin bowling alley looked much busier than the first time she had visited it with Sally. There were a few cars in the parking lot, along with several teenagers doing obnoxious teenager things under the glowing Madsen Candlepin

Lanes sign. Was that what she was like at that age? Actually, she'd rather not know.

Pushing through the double doors, Abigail stepped into the warmly lit den of Kirby Madsen's business. All eight lanes were in use by families and clusters of teens. The arcade also looked busy, but the bar only had a couple of chairs occupied.

Kirby was manning the bar, so Abigail made a beeline for an open seat. With his towering height, muscular physique, and disapproving-professor face, Kirby could come across as rather imposing. Even after getting to know him better, Abigail had no desire to ever fall on his bad side. But for now, she was very much on Kirby's good side after she had helped his brother reclaim the town's historic ship.

"Abigail," Kirby greeted her with his deep voice and slight accent. "What a pleasant surprise."

Was that sarcasm? Was he being genuine? Abigail could never tell with Kirby. Dag, Kirby's little brother and care-taker of the old whaling ship, the Lafayette, was an open book. He was fun and easygoing, and he never gave Sally too hard of a time about her eyeballing him from her store window while he worked on the ship. Kirby, on the other hand, was a hard nut to crack. Abigail sometimes wished he was a little less intimidating than his Viking ancestors.

"Nice to see you too, Kirby. Busy night."

Kirby grinned. At least, it looked like a grin. It could also have been a grimace. "Two birthdays."

Okay, well, Kirby was obviously not in the mood to chat.

If she wanted to find something out, she would have to ask him outright. "Kirby, I'm looking for someone."

"She's over there." He thrust his chin toward the arcade. "The one playing air hockey."

Abigail followed his gaze. At the air hockey table, a dark-haired woman was playing a game against a teenaged boy. A group of other boys surrounded the kid, gesturing excitedly at the table, at the woman, and at the ceiling. Abigail got the feeling he wasn't doing too well, and his friends were making sure he knew it.

"Wait." She whirled back around to face Kirby. "How did you know I was looking for Rachel?"

One corner of Kirby's mouth turned up in a crooked smile. It was mocking but not mean, and she felt like she was finally seeing a genuine emotion from the man, something other than aloofness or distrust. The smile didn't look bad on him. "You are like me, Abigail. You are suspicious. She is the only person here who might catch the attention of a suspecting person. And so that's how I know."

Abigail decided to take his comment as a compliment. "Thanks for the info, Kirby. Hope business keeps up."

Kirby shrugged. "Tourist season is almost here."

"Yeah," she sighed as she turned away. Grandma had said Abigail wouldn't be a true resident of Wallace Point until she had survived her first tourist season. Abigail looked forward to the challenge, though.

The air hockey game was just wrapping up as Abigail approached the table.

"I can't believe you lost to a girl," one of the boys taunted.

"Not just a girl," another chimed in. "A girl old enough to be your mom."

"Or your grandma!" added a third. The group sauntered away, voices cracking between peals of laughter.

"Charming, aren't they?" Rachel Cuthbert's voice was raspy and low as she pocketed a five—apparently a bet she had won just moments before.

Abigail wondered what kind of person had no qualms betting money against kids. Rachel stood quite tall next to Abigail, and her black leather boots made her even taller.

"Teens will be teens," Abigail offered as she studied the reporter. She had long brown hair with bangs that framed her dark, kohl-lined eyes, and she had a smile on her face that wasn't exactly friendly. She looked to be in her late 40s, about the same age as Abigail's mother.

Abigail decided to go for it. "I want to talk to you about the motel murder."

Rachel laughed. "At least you're more straight-forward than James was. That boy hasn't changed much. Still a kid playing a cop. You, on the other hand, I can't place. Familiar face though."

"You knew my mom. Sarah Lane."

That caught Rachel's attention. "Sarah, huh? You must be Abigail then."

"That's me."

"Do you know you look a lot like your grandmother did when she was young? I bet that really got to Sarah."

"Probably. So, do you have time for a few questions?"

"Not wasting a minute, are you?" Rachel eyed the air hockey table. "Well, why not? For the sake of an old friend. Let's step outside, though. I'm dying for a cigarette."

Abigail did not relish the idea of someone blowing cigarette smoke in her face, but she wasn't about to let Rachel out of her sight. So out they went.

Outside, Rachel lit a cigarette and took a long drag. After a moment, she asked, "So what do you want to know?"

"You apologized for claiming the Ripper was back."

"Yep."

"What made you think it was him?"

For the first time, Rachel's face became animated. "Are you kidding? I *hoped* it was him! We were selling copies like crazy during the Reginald Grimes case. To have the Ripper back again, to be the one to break the story, it would have been the most exciting thing to happen to this town, and to me."

"So you never had any good reason to suspect the Ripper?"

"Well, there was the stabbing. Those don't happen every day. How much do you know about the Wallace Point Ripper?"

"Not much," Abigail admitted.

Rachel smirked. "People don't like to talk about it often, but for years the Ripper was the terror of Wallace Point. Some people actually started to lock their doors. Can you believe that?"

Abigail shook her head. "Grandma only locks the door when I remind her."

Rachel pulled on her cigarette. "Yeah. Anyway, a pattern emerged after a few murders. The Ripper seemed to target upstanding citizens, the kind of people who made Wallace Point the quaint town we all know and love." Rachel shook her head, as if she couldn't understand what exactly there was to love about Wallace Point. Abigail could see why Rachel and her mom had gotten along.

Clusters of people began to pour out of the bowling alley. Kirby apparently was getting ready to close up.

Abigail pointed out, "But this victim wasn't from the Wallace Point community. He was an out-of-towner."

"Sure, but the Ripper hasn't been active in years, so I thought maybe this was a practice run before starting again in earnest. The injuries themselves were spot on. One stab wound to maim the victim so they couldn't get away. Those were usually on the lower body, like the Achilles heel. Another to hurt the victim. This was often the back, side, or stomach and involved a long laceration, hence the nickname the Ripper. And, finally, one stab straight through the heart. The Ripper was merciful in a way. A bit of pain and fear, but after that it was over pretty quickly for the victim."

Abigail shifted uncomfortably. Rachel had an odd sense of mercy. "And this victim had all three stab wounds?"

"Yeah, and the stab wounds were the same depth as the wounds the Ripper inflicted. The wounds might even have been made by the same weapon."

So far, it sounded like Rachel had good reason to suspect the Ripper. "So, why did you issue an apology?"

"The police didn't want to make a whole media circus about it, so I never got the full details until a few days ago. I knew about the injuries, knew about the possible similarities in the murder weapon, but the cops never confirmed if the killer did the ritual."

"Ritual?"

"The Ripper always burned candles. After he kills his victims, he lights a circle of candles around them. Whether he kills inside or outside, the victims are always within this circle. He did this every single time."

"And there were no candles at the crime scene."

"Not a one. Ended up making me look like a real idiot. Here I was, thinking that since the cops never confirmed or denied the existence of candles at the crime scene, that it *had* to be the Ripper. If it wasn't, why wouldn't the cops release that information? Oh well. It was a gamble, and I lost. Can't break a great story without taking risks."

Abigail mulled over the information as the last customers filed out of the bowling alley. She bought that Rachel could have jumped the gun, so to speak, with the lacking information she'd had. After all, there were some similarities.

But if the candle ritual was missing from the murder scene, why were the other details so similar? It couldn't be coincidence.

Rachel stomped on the butt of her cigarette. "Anyway, I'm going up to my apartment. Tell your mom I said hey."

Abigail could try. Her mom rarely called or answered her calls. "Will do. Thanks for your time, Rachel."

Rachel waved and headed up a metal staircase attached to the side of the building. Abigail turned slowly and set out toward home. She had a lot to think about on her short walk.

CHAPTER FIVE

Grandma was asleep by the time Abigail made it home. Thor, however, was waiting for her on the front porch. "Good old Thor," she said as she walked into the kitchen, her dog at her heels. "You won't let the Ripper catch me, will you?"

Hungry after her walk, she made herself a mug of steaming cocoa and a grilled cheese sandwich. She scarfed down the hot meal, washed up, then headed up to the bathroom for a quick shower.

When she emerged, she felt fresh and comfy, but not sleepy. Even worse, she felt too restless to sit down and open a book. So when Thor jumped up onto his side of the bed and settled in, Abigail didn't join him. Instead, she just stood and thought over the evening.

The conversation with Rachel had led to more questions

than answers. If the Ripper wasn't back, then who was the killer? And why would they choose to semi-imitate the Ripper?

Abigail was staring at nothing when an old box sitting in a corner of her room registered in her brain. It was the box of VHS tapes she had discovered in the attic. She'd kept it to take inventory of what other classics Grandma owned, but most of the tapes had been old home movies her mom had made. From the labels on the movies, it seemed to be footage of her mom and her old childhood friends, with names like 'Freddy,' 'Teddy,' 'Bobby,' 'Rachel,' 'Monica,' 'Sandy,' and so forth written on them with various years.

Abigail sighed. Why not take the box up now? Sure it was late, but she was restless anyway, so she might as well channel that energy toward something productive. And Grandma kept the attic as tidy as she kept her store, so it wasn't like Abigail would have to take another shower. Besides, standing in the middle of her room staring at the walls was getting her absolutely nowhere.

The spiral staircase up to the attic was in the hallway. She climbed the narrow winding stairs, holding the box tight under one arm. Abigail wasn't exactly a fan of wobbly steps combined with heights, but at least it wasn't a ladder.

The attic stretched over the whole house, but it was only just tall enough for Abigail to stand up if she hunched her shoulders. She tugged on a chain dangling right next to the stair landing and turned on a bare light bulb.

Grandma kept the space so organized that it only took a

minute to put the box back in the right spot, which was in the corner with an old television, projector, and record player.

Still restless, Abigail wandered to another corner full of cedar chests. She opened one chest and found dozens of romance paperbacks. Another chest was full of old toys. None of them were plastic, and they all looked like toys her mother would have called old-fashioned and hated.

The third chest was full of Wallace Point memorabilia. Nothing special, just trinkets picked up over various community festivals and events. She was just about to close the chest and move on to another when she spotted a photo album stuffed full of old newspaper clippings.

Acting on a hunch, Abigail pulled out the album and carried it over to the light of the bare bulb.

The first few articles were little announcements: people getting engaged, people getting married, people having babies. Then there was a grainy photo of Sarah playing Juliet in a school play. Abigail studied her mother's face. She looked happy, but not a nice happy. She seemed happy in the same way a kid who decimated an unsuspecting ant colony was happy.

The next article almost made Abigail drop the album. It was much older than the ones she had found during her initial search at the library. The headline read: *Wallace Point Ripper Claims Another Victim—Cassidy Wilson*. Abigail skipped down to the main article and started reading.

Last night, the body of Cassidy Wilson was discovered by her husband Sheriff William Wilson in the kitchen of their home. All details of the crime scene point to the work of the killer known as the Wallace Point Ripper. Sheriff Wilson was in the office, working late on another Ripper case. Their son, James, was staying with a friend.

Underneath the article was a photo of the little family. Sheriff Wilson looked like he was in his late 40s to early 50s. He stood tall and proud next to his wife and son. James, an adorable boy with big eyes and a head of unruly hair, looked like he was maybe eight or nine. Cassidy Wilson had been beautiful. She had big brown eyes, curly brown hair, and a smile that lit up her entire face.

So that was why Grandma had discouraged Abigail from discussing the case with Sheriff Wilson. Any mention of the Ripper must've been agony for him. He had been working on the case but had failed to solve it in time, and the price he had to pay was losing his wife to the same man he was trying to catch.

Abigail couldn't imagine what that felt like. Sure, she had no idea who her father was. And sure, her mom wasn't the greatest human on the planet. And, yeah, she hadn't even known her grandmother existed until about two months ago. But that wasn't anything like having the family you cherished ripped apart in such a gruesome way. No wonder the sheriff had been so exhausted and preoccupied a few days ago. And no wonder James decided to come back to support his father.

Abigail had to put down the album, her hands starting to shake. What the Ripper had done to Sheriff Wilson and his family was beyond horrible. And to have the past dredged up again like this? Sheriff Wilson might have lost his edge as a detective, but he was a good person and he didn't deserve to relive this nightmare.

Somehow Abigail had to get to the bottom of the motel stabbing. Otherwise Sheriff Wilson might never get to put his past behind him.

CHAPTER SIX

Much to Thor's disappointment, Abigail decided to skip their run the next morning. The past couple of days had been busy, and she was craving quality time with Grandma. Besides, she was hoping to glean some more information about Cassidy Wilson.

So, when Thor rolled onto her face to wake her up, she pushed him off and rolled onto him instead. Once she felt he'd had enough of being a living pillow, she got dressed and headed downstairs to make breakfast.

Abigail wasn't an incredible cook, but Grandma had pancake mix and a waffle maker. She whipped the batter together and let it sit for a few minutes while she whisked eggs and put some bacon in the oven. Once the bacon reached peak crispiness, Abigail drained most of the fat from the baking sheet into a little jar, reserving the rest to cook the scrambled eggs.

While the coffee was brewing, Abigail sliced frozen strawberries and mixed them with a tablespoon of sugar so they would juice. Then she whipped some heavy cream and set it on the table with butter, real maple syrup, and chocolate chips.

"Aren't you up and at 'em today!" Grandma yawned from the kitchen doorway. She was still dressed in her long flannel nightgown and slippers. "What's that delicious smell?"

Coffee in hand, Abigail crossed the room to kiss her grandmother on the cheek and hand her a steaming mug. "Breakfast."

"Thank you, dearest. I'll be back. I need to let Missy out to take care of her business."

"Sure thing. I'll finish up in here."

Soon they all took their places at the table to eat the feast. Missy and Thor sat a respectable distance away from the table and watched them eat with long, sad expressions on their furry faces.

"What's the occasion?" Grandma asked as she buttered her first waffle.

"No occasion. I just missed you so I thought I'd skip my run and make us breakfast."

"I'm glad you did. You sure know how to keep an old lady plump and rosy."

They ate in silence for a few minutes, savoring each other's company and the flavors on their plates. Abigail was the first to speak again. "So, Grandma. I went up to the attic last night to put away the box of VHS tapes."

"Oh, thank you for doing that. Climbing those steep spiral stairs is harder than it used to be. Let me guess, you looked around and found something interesting?"

"Well, yeah. How'd you know?"

"Deductive reasoning. I have a very interesting attic and a curious granddaughter who obviously had excess energy last night. Tell me, what did you find?"

Abigail shifted in her seat. Why did she feel like she had done something wrong? She had done a little poking around, but nothing Grandma would disapprove of. "I found a news-paper clipping about Cassidy Wilson."

Grandma tilted her head in thought. "Was it the clipping with her recipe for chocolate pie?"

"N-no."

"Was it about the time she saved a tourist from choking on a jumbo shrimp?"

"No."

Grandma's face grew serious, and her usually bright eyes dimmed. "Was it about her murder?"

Abigail simply nodded. Now she really did feel like she had done something wrong. Maybe she shouldn't have brought it up, especially over breakfast. Way to ruin a lovely start to the morning...

Grandma continued, "Not even thinking about the pain she and her family went through, do you want to know what makes my blood boil?"

Abigail nodded.

"The murder is how we remember Cassidy now. No one remembers her chocolate pie or how she saved that tourist. The Ripper didn't just kill her. He erased who she was."

"Grandma, I'm sorry. I shouldn't have brought this up."

"No, dear, that's all right. Why is this on your mind?"

Abigail hesitated. She had obviously brought up some tough memories for Grandma. Why keep inflicting more pain? "Never mind, Grandma. Forget I said anything. Let me tell you more about the coffee party with Sally. You would have loved it."

For the rest of breakfast, the two simply caught up. They ate their waffles and sipped their coffee. Abigail detailed everything she had learned from Sally about tea etiquette. Grandma told her about the shenanigans the Granny Gang was planning for the winter tourist season. Missy and Thor contributed a huff or a sneeze here and there.

By the time the last bite of crispy bacon was savored, Abigail finally felt caught up on the quality Grandma time she'd been craving. She washed the dishes while Grandma tidied the kitchen.

Lethargic after the large meal and relaxed by the homey morning, Abigail found herself feeling profoundly grateful for her quiet little life with Grandma. But she couldn't help thinking about Sheriff Wilson and the horror he was reliving. If even mentioning Cassidy Wilson had been so hard for Grandma, how much worse was this case for the sheriff?

Then another thought struck her. A month had passed

since the murder, but the case hadn't been solved. The rest of Wallace Point had rejected the claims that the Ripper was back. But had Willy Wilson? Perhaps, in his mind, this might've been his last chance to catch the Ripper. Abigail couldn't help but wonder if his tragic experience might blind him to the possibility that the Ripper wasn't to blame this time.

GRANDMA AND ABIGAIL geared themselves up for another slow morning. Thor, after a long look at his leash, parked himself on the front porch. Missy settled underneath Grandma's feet. It was another cool day, so they left the door wide open to welcome the breeze. They each picked up a book, and the ocean took care of their background music.

A little before noon, Bobby Kent paid them an unexpected visit. Today he wore a baby blue leisure suit with a black turtleneck. "Good morning!" he announced, as if they had just won a new car. He shot them with his finger guns. "How are you ravishing ladies doing on this magnificent day?"

"Bobby Kent," Grandma said, a sparkle in her eyes. "No one has ever called me ravishing before."

"Well, they should have, because it is absolutely true, Florence."

She laughed. "What brings you by today? A gift for Sally, perhaps?"

"You know, that's a marvelous idea. But I came for one of your fantastic cookies."

"Then help yourself! Just remember the rules."

"How could I forget? Do you have any suggestions?"

Abigail jumped up from her chair. "I know just the thing, Bobby. Give me one second." She left Bobby with Grandma at the counter while she hunted through the store, but she could still clearly hear their conversation.

"Any news in Wallace Point?" Grandma asked.

"Well," said Bobby, ever the gossip. "Not so much in Wallace Point, but I heard tell of an oddity in Turtle Bay."

"The next town over? Did you know they're on the lookout for an old ship to rival the Lafayette?"

"They won't find one. Nothing beats the Lafayette's history here, especially after that treasure was found. But that's not the news I'm talking about."

Grandma gasped. "By all means, do tell."

"It could be related to the motel stabbing."

Abigail froze just as she found what she was looking for. She held her breath, waiting for Bobby to continue.

"A wedding was canceled in Turtle Point. Doesn't sound like much, right? I thought the same thing. It is regrettable, but not unheard of, for a bride or a groom to get cold feet. But listen to this: The murder happened the day before the wedding was supposed to kick off."

"I don't know, Bobby. That's not much to go off of."

"There's more. The bride and groom had booked a hotel in Turtle Bay for their out-of-town guests, but when the guests arrived, there weren't enough rooms to go around. They had to scramble for lodging and apparently some of them checked into that dreadful motel at the edge of town. The same motel where the murder took place."

In the silence that followed, Abigail decided her absence might start to look suspicious. So she picked up the clunky antique and carried it back to the counter.

Grandma broke into a smile. "Abigail, that is perfect! Why hadn't I thought of that before?"

Bobby Kent peered at the item. Then he pulled his glasses out of his suit pocket and peered again. "What is it?"

"It's an antique wall-mounted coffee grinder," Abigail said. "The glass container at the top holds the coffee beans. When you're ready for fresh ground coffee, you turn this iron crank here. The grounds fall into this little glass jar down here, which you can unscrew and carry to your coffee maker."

"Now just look at that." Bobby's wide grin matched Grandma's. "Sally is going to love this! Thank you, Abigail. I'm going to get extra brownie points for this one."

"No problem, Bobby." Abigail wrapped the grinder in newspaper and placed it in a bag. Maybe she was starting to pick up on some of Grandma's excellent sales tactics.

After Bobby paid for the gift and left, it was time to close for lunch. Abigail didn't feel very hungry. What she really wanted to do was go to the library and look over all the newspaper articles related to the stabbing again.

Bobby's gossip had sparked lots of questions in her mind.

Could the victim have been one of the wedding guests? That would certainly be a good reason to cancel a wedding. And if that were the case, was it possible the murderer was actually another guest?

To Thor's delight, Abigail picked up his leash. "Grandma, I think I'm going to take Thor for a quick walk, then I'm going to head to the library. Do you mind?"

"Not at all, honey. After that perfect sale to Bobby, you deserve a break."

"Thanks, Grandma. I'll be back in a bit." She leashed Thor and headed out the door. The sun was shining, the day was warming up, and the breeze was refreshing, but Abigail was so preoccupied with her thoughts that she didn't really notice any of it.

She also didn't notice the man on the sidewalk just outside the store parking lot. At least, not until she walked right into him.

The impact was so hard that she stumbled back and fell onto her bottom.

"Ow!" she yelped, looking up to see the brick wall of a man she ran into.

The perpetrator was a tall, dark stranger, yet something was familiar about him. It only took Abigail a second to recognize the big brown eyes and unruly brown hair she had seen in that old newspaper clipping.

James Wilson.

CHAPTER SEVEN

James peered down at Abigail, not bothering to offer her a hand. He looked only mildly surprised that he had just rammed into her, and merely said, "Whoops. You okay there, Cupcake?"

Abigail blinked. "Cupcake? Who's a cupcake?"

"You, I suppose."

Abigail wasn't sure how to take being called such a cute nickname by someone who was basically a complete stranger. "Listen here, buddy. The name's Abigail, *not* Cupcake."

James looked around. "Oh. But you're as small as a cupcake. I hardly saw you."

Some detective this guy was. "I'm walking a Great Dane. How do you miss that?"

James shrugged, a smirk slowly spreading across his face. "I missed the dog too. He's rather small for a Great Dane."

Abigail frowned. Thor was massive. Was James trying to evoke a reaction out of her? Because, well, he was succeeding.

She looked over at her Great Dane. "Thor, why don't you escort this gentleman off Grandma's yard?"

Thor seemed to nod as he stepped between James and Abigail, giving the man a long, menacing stare. James blinked, then held out his hand for Thor to sniff.

Thor took one step forward, sniffed James's hand...

Then he wagged his tail.

"Ugh!" Abigail groaned as she watched James kneel and ruffle Thor's floppy ears. The dog started licking his face silly, sending the man into laughter.

And here Abigail thought Lee Lebeau gave bad first impressions. She was just about to open her mouth and utter the words, "You're banned from the store—*forever!*" when Grandma popped her head out of her front door.

"Abigail? Everything all right? Oh, I see you've met James!"

Abigail gave Thor's leash a little yank and grumbled, "Yeah, I've met him, all right. Real charmer."

James winked at Abigail then headed up the porch stairs to give Grandma a hug. When he turned to see Abigail following right behind him, he asked, "Weren't you just on your way out?"

"Change of plans," Abigail said evenly, not about to leave James unattended with her grandmother.

Inside the store, Grandma stood on her tiptoes to pinch James's cheek. "So good to see you, James. What do you think of my beautiful granddaughter, Abigail?"

"She reminds me of you when you were younger," James said, a sparkle in his eyes.

Abigail sighed and nodded, not about to refuse that compliment.

Grandma handed James a cookie and asked, "How is your dear father holding up?"

James took a small bite before shaking his head. "This case has him on edge. I don't think he's getting much sleep."

Abigail studied James. He was tall like his father, with a strong jaw and broad shoulders. His brown hair spilled into his eyes, and he was in need of a shave. With his trench coat and wrinkled clothing, he definitely looked the part of a dodgy PI from the big city.

James continued, "It's a tough case. There are some similarities to the old Ripper cases, but it doesn't line up perfectly, so we're still at a loss."

Abigail saw her chance to possibly connect some dots. "Yeah, I was just talking to Rachel about it earlier. You know, the reporter? She still seems pretty convinced it's the Ripper, despite her walking back her story. What do you make of that?"

James blinked. He must not have expected Abigail to have done some investigating on her own. Once he gained his composure, he said, "Rachel's a whole other can of worms. All she's done is muddy up the case, taking what are mere coincidences and running with them."

Abigail wasn't convinced. "I don't believe in coincidences."

"Well, then, assume it's a copycat. Or someone pretending to be a copycat."

"Why would someone pretend to be a copycat?"

"You tell me, Nancy Drew."

"James," Grandma cut in with her best sweet old lady voice. "Would you like another cookie?"

He looked down at the first one she had handed him. "Um. That's okay. I'm still enjoying this one, and I don't think I can afford to buy two antiques."

"Oh, James!" Grandma laughed, waving him off sheepishly. "You've always been so silly. You know you get free cookies… as long as you tell us what we want to know." Her face suddenly grew serious.

James choked a little on the last bite of his cookie. He looked away, before turning a pair of dark, earnest eyes back to Abigail and Grandma. "Listen, I heard you helped with the Reginald Grimes murder. That's great. Good job there. But you don't want to get involved in this mess. Trust me, lay off this one."

Grandma chuckled. "My granddaughter's quite persistent, much like me."

James nodded. "Yeah, I can see that. Well, it's been great meeting you, Abigail, and seeing you, Granny, but I really gotta go. I'll stop by again soon." James turned to leave, then paused to nod at Thor, who was sitting next to the door. Thor gave him a friendly *ruff*, to which James said, "Good boy," before he headed out.

Once he was gone, Abigail grumbled at Thor, "Traitor. You're supposed to have my back. You know, strike fear into the hearts of my enemies, that sort of thing? Not kiss them!"

Thor yawned and trotted off to the kitchen to eat his kibble. Abigail turned to Grandma. "Can you believe he just told us to lay off this case? I could understand his father maybe telling us that, but James has no more authority than either of us."

Grandma gave her a knowing look. "So we're on a case, are we?"

Abigail remembered how much Grandma didn't want to relive her Ripper memories. "We're not. I'm just… worried, is all. Call me a concerned citizen."

"Okay, so which of the leads should we follow first?"

"Leads? You mean you want to investigate the case?"

"Murder's bad for business. The sooner we solve this, the sooner my sales go back up."

Abigail smiled. "Always the capitalist. But what did you mean by *which* of the leads?"

"Well, we have a few possibilities, don't we? First, there's the possibility that this really is the Ripper. Heaven forbid that's the case. Then, there's the possibility that this is a copycat. Someone could be trying to use the cold case to distract the police. And then, your least favorite possibility, the similarities could simply be pure coincidence."

"No way. Something tells me this isn't a coincidence, Grandma."

"I feel the same way. So, how do we want to go about this?"

"Well, before James showed up, I was going to revisit the library after walking Thor. When I first visited the library, I only looked up articles from the past few months. Now I'm thinking I should read up on older reports from when the Ripper was still active."

"That's a good start."

"Yeah. And when I get back, maybe we could go to that motel, see if we can find out anything there. After what Bobby said, I'm starting to think this wedding drama might be relevant to the murder case."

"That's a great place to start. I know the motel owner, Mary Chang. She's an odd one, but she'll talk to me." Grandma paused, nodding as she plotted their next steps. "How's this for a plan? I'll man the store on the off-chance we get a sale this afternoon, while you go to the library and read everything you can about the Ripper murders. It's time you knew the history. Goodness knows the rest of this town can't forget it. When you're done, meet me here and we'll go see Mary."

"Brilliant, Grandma. I'll see you then." Abigail gave her a quick peck on her soft cheek and grabbed her coat before heading out.

This time, Abigail walked with a spring in her step. It felt surprisingly good to start on another case, despite the dark details. It felt especially good to join forces with Grandma. Grandma was a wealth of information, but more than that, Abigail treasured going on any kind of adventure with her grandmother.

CHAPTER EIGHT

Abigail squirmed in the hard wooden chair at the cubicle in the library. When she had asked the librarian for help accessing older newspaper articles from the Ripper's heyday, she had expected to be taken to a lonely basement filled with old filing cabinets. Instead, the librarian had parked her at the same bulky desktop computer she had used last time.

Scrolling on the computer might not have been as fun as flipping through crumbling pages, but it sure was faster. After a few hours, Abigail had read all there was to read from the local newspapers about the Ripper's original murders, dating all the way back to 1990.

Abigail logged off the computer, stood up, and stretched. The library was as quiet as a graveyard; the librarian drifted from shelf to shelf like a ghost. With a silent wave, Abigail stepped out of the musty building into the sun and fresh air.

After spending hours pent up indoors, Abigail appreciated the walk home. The day was gorgeous, and the light exercise revived her body and her mind.

Two months ago she had been a claims adjuster, walking around a crowded, noisy city as she chased after potential fraudsters. Her interactions with both customers and management were often less than pleasant, and her reward at the end of the day was the traffic of the big city.

Now, she knew most of her customers by name, her grandmother was her manager, and she never had to deal with traffic. She couldn't believe her good luck and felt grateful about living in such a nice, quiet town. She also tried her best to ignore the approaching tourist season.

Grandma was ready and waiting by the time Abigail made it home. "Good, you're early," she said. "I packed us some sandwiches. Oh, and I've called Mary to let her know we're coming. She likes to be warned, you know. If we just showed up, she would tell us she was too busy."

"Great! I learned a lot at the library. I don't know if any of it will be useful for this case, but it certainly can't hurt. By the way…" Abigail stopped, reaching out to touch Grandma's shoulder. "I'm sorry about everything you and the town had to go through with the Ripper."

Grandma took in a sharp breath, caught off guard by the turn in conversation. To Abigail's surprise, Grandma's eyes misted over briefly. "Thank you, dear. That was a terrible time for everybody, something we thought we had put behind us. Now this case pops up, dragging all of those old memories back up." She shook her head. The tears disappeared just as quickly as they came. A look of determination took their place. "Let's catch ourselves a murderer, shall we?"

Abigail nodded and gave Grandma a big, loving hug.

THEY ATE their sandwiches in the car. Grandma had really gone all out with them: crusty sourdough bread spread with an olive salad, layers of extra sharp cheese, and thin slices of salty salami. To complement it, they drank hot black tea out of thermoses.

The drive to the motel was a little over fifteen minutes, and Abigail found it vaguely familiar. Soon, she figured out why.

"Grandma, I've checked into this motel before."

"When?"

"When you were in a coma in the hospital. I booked this place and checked in before I came to see you. Then I met Sally in your hospital room, and she said I shouldn't stay here. She called it a 'roach motel.' So I checked out quickly after that."

They pulled up to the motel. Several two-story buildings encircled around an empty parking lot. The exteriors of the buildings had been painted a soft white, blooming shrubs hugged the clean sidewalks, and the pavement had been recently resurfaced.

"It doesn't look too roachy on the outside," Grandma commented. "Let's see about the inside."

The lobby was just as neat and welcoming. The room looked fresh and clean, with plants decorating the corners. The check-in desk was simple and unobtrusive. There were even a couple of miniature fountains tucked around the guest waiting chairs. The place felt more like a living room than a lobby.

A small, dark haired woman bustled up behind the check-in desk. She had piercing eyes which she cast sharply at Abigail and Grandma, giving no indication that she had ever seen either. "Yes?"

"Hello, Mary." Grandma stepped forward. "How are you?"

"Fine. How are you?"

"Well, I'm just fine. This is my granddaughter, Abigail. She was a guest here not too long ago. Or, almost a guest."

Mary squinted at Abigail. "Yes. You checked in and one hour later checked out. You didn't pay."

Abigail froze. "Er, I thought… I mean, I was told I didn't have to pay."

"That's right."

"Oh. Well, good." Abigail found little Mary Chang rather intimidating. She was surprised anyone would even consider committing a crime under her roof, much less actually commit it.

Grandma took over the conversation again. "Thank you for taking the time to talk to us about the murder, Mary."

Mary's face turned from sour to threatening. "Murder. In my motel. As if I wasn't having a hard enough time with this place."

"What do you mean?" Abigail dared to ask.

"What do you mean what do I mean? Do you know what people called this place before the murder?"

"Oh, um, no. No, I don't think so."

"A roach motel! Roaches! As if I would ever stand roaches. There hasn't been a roach in this motel for over five years, ever since I took it over from the previous owner. I bought it. I cleaned it. I had a bug man spray it. In fact, the bug man still sprays it every month. Did anyone notice? No. They still called it a roach motel."

"What about since the murder?"

"Since? Ha! Even worse. Now they call it a murder motel. It's bad for business!"

"You're telling me!" Grandma said, seeing her opportunity and taking it. "Business at my antique store has been next to nothing lately. So please, Mary, tell us anything you can, and we'll try to put an end to this mess."

Mary glared at Grandma and Abigail. Finally she sighed, and her tense face relaxed. "I've told the police everything and they still haven't caught the Ripper. Might as well try something new."

"Miss Chang," Abigail began. She didn't feel comfortable

calling Mary by her first name. "You think the Ripper did this?"

Mary nodded. "Yes. Absolutely."

Abigail and Grandma glanced at each other. "May I ask why you think it was the Ripper?"

"Yes, of course, ask whatever you like. I know it's the Ripper because he dressed like the Ripper. And I overheard the police say it's the same knife used in the original murders. Who else could it be?"

"Wait, he dressed like him? You mean you saw him?"

"Yes. I have surveillance cameras around the buildings. The police took the tapes as evidence, but trust me, I saw him with my own eyes."

Grandma asked, "How exactly did he dress, Mary?"

"Like the grim reaper. Black hoodie, pants, everything."

Grandma looked at Abigail. "Does that match what the newspapers said about the original murders?"

Abigail recalled what she had read, "He wasn't caught on camera back then, but some people reported seeing a figure dressed in black near the crime scenes." Abigail turned to Mary. "Miss Chang, did the cameras catch where he came from? Or, could he have been a guest here?"

Mary shook her head. "The cameras can see the guest room doors, the parking lot, and some of the woods behind the buildings. The video showed him coming out of the woods. He came on foot, so there's no way to know what car he might have been driving."

Grandma tried a different line of questioning. "What can you tell us about the guest who was murdered?"

"Well, he was never supposed to stay here. He came with a group of others who had been invited to a wedding. The hotel the wedding party had reserved, the Turtle Heights, overbooked." Mary rolled her eyes. "Can you believe that name? It's a one-story motel! And they overbook all the time too. Anyway, he was part of that crowd. I remember him, actually. He was a rude, rude man."

"What did he look like?"

"Middle-aged. Used to be a resident of Wallace Point. He mentioned that all his 'good old days' happened in this town when he was younger. A lot of those guests came from regions around Wallace Point."

"Where are these guests now?" Grandma asked.

"Long gone. Well, since the wedding was canceled, they only stuck around for as long as the police made them stay."

"Do you have any of their names, Miss Chang? It might be helpful to talk to a couple of them."

Mary frowned. "I gave their names to the police. I'd rather keep them confidential from anyone else. It's bad for business, disrespecting my guests' privacy."

"I understand completely, Mary." Grandma put on her charming old lady voice. "Is there anything else you think we should know?"

"Did I already mention the wedding was canceled?"

"Yes, Miss Chang."

"Then, no, I don't think so. Oh! Wait. There was an odd

man who wanted to buy anything the victim left in his room."

Both Grandma and Abigail started, and Abigail pressed further, "Any idea who he is?"

Mary shrugged. "No, he was very pushy. I didn't like him one bit. I told him to get out."

Abigail sighed. "Well, did you tell the police about him?"

"Why would I? I don't bother them with every weirdo who propositions me. You meet lots of weirdos in the hospitality business. Just part of the job. He left an email address though, in case I change my mind. Which I won't."

"Mary," Grandma said gently, "would you give us that email? He might know something."

ABIGAIL AND GRANDMA piled into the car fairly satisfied with their afternoon's work.

Abigail began, "So, we confirmed that Bobby's story about the canceled wedding was spot on."

"I knew you were eavesdropping!"

"Of course I was, Grandma," Abigail said with a grin. "I wouldn't be a proper Wallace Point resident if I wasn't an expert eavesdropper, now would I? Anyhow, we've also confirmed what Rachel Cuthbert told me about the injuries. As Miss Chang overheard, the police were saying it's possible the killer used the very same knife as the Ripper. I don't know how that's possible unless it really is the Ripper."

Grandma shuddered. "Abigail, I have a feeling you're not going to like this, but we need to tell James about the guy who wanted the victim's belongings."

"What? Grandma, no way!"

"Now dear, just hear me out."

Abigail tightened her grip on the steering wheel. There was no way she was going to let that rude PI get his hands on her hard work. Not even Grandma could convince her!

CHAPTER NINE

I t didn't take long for Grandma to convince Abigail, and by the time they were home, it had been decided. In the battle of wills between Grandma and Abigail, Grandma always won. Abigail knew her tricks better than anyone, and still she wasn't immune to them. Her granny was just too darn adorable.

Besides, Abigail had to admit that the police might've been able to use the information. If they talked to James first, he could decide whether the email address should be phoned in to Sheriff Wilson.

Back at the store, Grandma handed Abigail a folded scrap of paper.

"What's this?" Abigail asked.

"It's James's phone number. He gave it to me when I went

to visit him just after he came back to town. Be a dear and call him over."

"No way! You should be the one to call him. He knows you better."

"Oh, honey." Grandma's voice became inexplicably shaky, as if she had suddenly aged twenty years. She reached down gingerly to pet Thor and Missy. "I'm just so worn out from today. I need to sit and rest for a minute. Be a sweetheart and help your grandmother out."

"But Grandma," Abigail complained. Grandma blinked up at her, sudden fatigue all over her sweet face. Abigail sighed. "Oh, all right."

"Thank you, darling, thank you. I'll just rest right here." Grandma perched herself behind the checkout counter. She propped her elbows up on the smooth surface, cradled her angelic face in her hands, and stared at Abigail expectantly.

Abigail whipped out her phone and punched in James's phone number. The phone rang. Then it rang again. Then it kept on ringing until Abigail was sure the line was disconnected or out of range.

Just when she was about to hang up, the other line picked up. James gasped into her ear as if someone had just socked him in the stomach. "Hello?"

"Are you all right?"

"Yes." More strangled breaths for air. "Yes, I'm fine."

"Jeez, what are you doing? Chasing down a paramour?"

The gasping paused. "Paramour? Who is this?"

"Abigail Lane. Grandma wants you to come to the store."

"Ah, Cupcake!" James's voice sounded pleased, though still just as winded. "Nope, I'm not chasing down any soon-to-be divorcées. I'm just going for a jog. Speaking of which, we should run together sometime. Camille tells me you're quite the athlete."

Abigail could hear the teasing tone in his voice. She gripped the phone tighter, trying to keep her cool in front of Grandma. "My name is not Cupcake. Grandma requests your presence at the store. Should we be expecting you?"

"I feel like I'm being invited to a ball. Sure, I'll come. Give me twenty minutes. Will there be cookies?"

"I guess you'll have to see for yourself." Abigail hung up, not about to ask her exhausted grandmother to go bake something right now... "He's coming."

"Oh! Lovely!" Grandma sprang up. "I'll go make some cookies. Why don't you go freshen up?"

"What? Why? James was on a run. He's probably going to show up super sweaty. And don't trouble yourself with cooking. We don't need to feed everyone who comes by."

"Now, Abigail, you know I take care of my guests. I'll bake the cookies while you go on upstairs and get cleaned up. I can't have you possibly seeing my secret recipe anyhow." With that, Grandma all but danced her way into the kitchen.

Abigail shook her head as she and Thor headed upstairs. She had known, of course she had known, that Grandma's sudden fatigue had been an act. Just like she knew all about Grandma's secret cookie recipe.

Not long after moving in, Abigail had discovered Grandma pulling out a tub of store-bought cookie dough from the fridge. They had both decided to pretend it never happened, and since then, Abigail had been keeping the terrible secret locked deep down in her heart, never to be known by another Wallace Point citizen.

WHEN ABIGAIL CAME BACK down the stairs, her skin smelled like soap, the house smelled like cookies, and Grandma was whistling a happy little tune.

Someone knocked on the door just then. Grandma was still in the kitchen, and Abigail was closer anyway. She sighed, motioned for Thor to come with her, and went to unlock the door.

James stood there, his drab gray shirt clinging to his skin, and tendrils of wet brown hair clinging to his face. "Hey, Cupcake!" Catching sight of the Great Dane standing stoically at Abigail's side, he added, "Good boy, Thor."

Thor woofed in response as Abigail stepped back to let James inside. "Why do you insist on calling me that?"

"What?"

"Cupcake."

"I don't know." James flashed her a bright smile. "Once I get into a habit, it's hard to break."

Abigail rolled her eyes. "It's a day-old habit. I think you can break it." She then led the way to the kitchen.

"James!" Grandma exclaimed as they entered the kitchen. "Thank you so much for coming. Sit down and have a cookie."

Grandma had set three places at the table. Each place had a mug of steaming hot cocoa topped with giant marshmallows. There were also heaping bowls of shepherd's pie and small plates of salad. In the center of the table was a platter piled high with fresh cookies.

"Grandma!" Abigail said, her mouth watering just at the sight of the food. "When did you make all this? I was upstairs for fifteen minutes!"

"I made it this afternoon, while you were at the library. Today has just been the longest day, hasn't it? Anyhow, all I had to do was reheat the pie, throw some greens on a plate, and whip up hot cocoa. It's elementary, really."

James eased himself into a chair. "Granny Lane, I can't tell you how excited I am about this meal. My dad isn't exactly a genius in the kitchen."

"I'm sure you're right." Grandma sank down next to him and pinched his arm. "Now, we're going to have to make this quick. I'm just about ready for bed. Go ahead, Abigail. Tell him what we've learned."

Abigail filled James in on their afternoon visit to Mary Chang's motel, and told him about the creep who had left an email address.

James groaned. "Must be that fan club."

"Fan club?" Abigail asked.

"There are people out there who make rock stars out of serial killers. It's demented if you ask me."

"It is in bad taste," Grandma agreed. "And it really is too soon. But, to be fair, it's not unheard of. In the antiques world, items related to Bonnie and Clyde, Billy the Kid, and so on are very popular items."

"That may be, but Billy the Kid's victims didn't die a month ago, Granny Lane. They ought to wait until those who were close to the victims are long gone. But there's no accounting for decency." James's jaw tightened. "The guy who left the email address? Yeah, I have a feeling it's the punk who has the original Wallace Point Ripper knife."

Abigail gasped despite herself. "He has the murder weapon? How do you know?"

"A long time ago it was taken out of the evidence room at the station and sold on the black market. Can you believe there's a black market anywhere near Wallace Point? Eventually the knife ended up in his hands, though the police haven't ever been able to get it back from him. We don't have definitive proof, but he certainly seems to have it. He calls himself a 'murderabilia' collector. Collects memorabilia of murderers."

"Wait." Abigail frowned. "So the police know who this guy is and they know he has the weapon. Why aren't they going after him?"

"Like I said, we don't have definitive proof, and he hasn't been very cooperative. He fancies himself an amateur policeman too. 'Knows his rights,' and all that hullabaloo."

Abigail fell silent, finding it ironic that James would call someone else an amateur policeman. James took the lull as an opportunity to stuff more shepherd's pie into his mouth. Grandma, despite her obvious interest, looked like she could fall asleep at any moment. But Abigail was brooding.

"It sounds like the police need our help on this one," she said at last.

"Oh yeah?" James finished chewing his food. "What advantage do you have over this guy that the police don't?"

"Well, for one thing, I'm not a police officer. If this guy thinks I'm a regular person, or better yet, a potential customer, he might talk to me."

"Abigail, dear, what are you suggesting?"

"I don't know exactly, Grandma. But what if..." Abigail was thinking fast. "What if I pretend to be interested in one of his pieces? I could email him and, you know, just try to meet him and get him talking."

James wiped his mouth with a napkin. "Hey Cupcake, I think you just had a bright idea."

"Thanks, James. I do have those every so often."

He grinned. "But what if instead of being interested in something he might have, you offered him what we already know he wants: the bloody shirt of the recent murder victim. It's in the evidence room. I can get a picture of it to send to our collector."

"Right. Then once we have a time and a place to meet the guy, we can turn the tables on him, try to find out whatever he knows."

"Oh, Abigail, I don't know," Grandma interjected. "This sounds awfully risky."

Abigail reached out to touch Grandma's hand. "It is a bit risky. I admit that. But I think it might help crack this case. We can't let someone continue to get away with murder, not to mention what this is doing to Sheriff Wilson."

Grandma frowned, then nodded.

"It's a plan then," James said, reaching for a cookie.

CHAPTER TEN

Abigail stared at her email, feeling half-impressed with herself and half-repulsed by the memorabilia collector. The first email she'd sent had simply stated she had a rare item she wanted to sell, and that she had heard he might be interested. Abigail figured he was cautious in his line of work and would be more willing to work with someone who was equally cautious.

He had responded just as discreetly, confirming he was a collector of rare items. He wanted to know what type of rarity she could offer. The guy never gave his name, never betrayed anything about himself.

Abigail followed his lead. In her next email, she asked whether he had heard about the motel murder on the outskirts of Wallace Point. With some hesitation, Abigail had attached the photo of the bloody shirt James had provided.

She was careful to share nothing about who she could be, except that she was female and on the younger side, in hopes of lowering his guard.

The creep took the bait. He'd made an offer, an offer which Abigail automatically refused. She didn't know the first thing about the dollar value of murder memorabilia, but she did know that when someone made any kind of offer, it never hurt to ask for more, and that'd make her seem more legitimate.

The collector accepted her counteroffer and gave her a date, time, and location. Then came the real risk—revealing that Abigail would be accompanied by a man. Two people were more intimidating than one, so the guy might get cold feet at the unexpected change in the agreement.

To soften the blow, she claimed the man was her boyfriend and that he was the real connection to the evidence. She hadn't told James that detail; she didn't plan to tell him, either. She was pretty sure James would use the information to tease her, and he had given her a hard enough time already.

Then, for a full day, Abigail sat on pins and needles, waiting for the guy to reply. Once he finally did, she grabbed her phone and dialed James's number. When he picked up, Abigail said, "We're on."

GRANDMA HANDED James and Abigail sandwiches and two

thermoses of steaming coffee as they stood on the front porch of the store. "Now, you two be careful," Grandma told them, looking up at the gray skies. "If anything seems odd, just get out of there."

"Don't worry," Abigail said, kissing her grandmother's cheek. "We'll stay on our toes."

James, with a small black duffel bag slung over one shoulder, threw an arm around Grandma's small frame and drew the older woman in for a gentle hug. "Yeah, Granny Lane. Don't worry. I'll watch out for your granddaughter."

Grandma gave him a wry smile. "Abigail knows how to watch out for herself. But I appreciate it, James."

"Okay, let's get going," Abigail broke in. "We don't want to be late for our rendezvous."

The collector had chosen a location far outside Wallace Point. James and Abigail were essentially embarking on a mini-road trip to the middle of nowhere.

The remote location hadn't surprised James one bit. To him, it made sense that the collector didn't want to give strangers any idea where he lived.

Though James had showed up in his own vehicle, Abigail insisted that they take her car. She wanted to have as much control as possible over the situation she was about to get into.

She wasn't afraid, though. Grandma knew where she was headed and with whom. Abigail was going to give her a call when they arrived at the rendezvous, and then again when they were about to leave.

James believed the confrontation wouldn't take long, so if more than twenty minutes passed without a second call, Grandma would notify Sheriff Wilson.

Overall, Abigail felt like they had taken a decent amount of precautions. Now it was time to implement the plan.

It began to rain as they pulled out of the parking lot, and Abigail found herself wishing she could've taken Thor with her. The Great Dane sat on the porch beside Grandma, watching with big, mopey eyes as she drove away. She would have brought him, but she didn't like the idea of leaving Grandma alone when there was a killer on the loose.

James turned on the radio to an oldies station. Sinatra's velvety voice poured into the car, crooning about the life he'd lived. James grinned. "You're in luck, Cupcake."

Clutching one hand to his chest and swinging the other out in front of him, as if gesturing to an immense crowd, he joined right in with Sinatra. "I did what I had to do," he sang, his voice surprisingly good and understated. "And saw it through without exemption."

"Um," Abigail said. "No." She switched off the radio.

James feigned disbelief. "You don't like my singing, Cupcake? But everyone tells me I'm a great singer."

"Clearly I'm not everyone. And it's Abigail."

"But Cupcake suits you." James leaned back in his chair with an exaggerated sigh. "You're so much like Granny Lane when she was younger. I grew up with her, you know."

Abigail shook her head. "Can't help but admit I'm a little

envious. I didn't even know she was still around until recently."

"I'm sorry to hear that. I will admit I was a little curious why you never visited her."

"I have my mom to thank for that. She got upset at Grandma over something stupid, and that apparently was enough to keep me out of Grandma's life."

"Man, that had to be hard."

Part of Abigail was bothered that he had known Grandma far longer than she had. Though she tried not to dwell on a past she couldn't change, she regretted all the years they had missed.

Her curiosity got the best of her. "What was she like? When you were a kid, I mean."

"Well, she went through a rough patch when… you know, your mom and grandfather left her. I was pretty young. I really only remember that one day she had a daughter and a husband, and the next day she didn't. And that she was sad for a while. I remember that because her cookies didn't taste quite the same. This was, of course, back when Granny used to give cookies away, before she had a store and started using them to extort her customers."

Abigail thought about the premade cookie dough in the refrigerator at home. And she thought about how awful Grandma must have felt when she had lost her family overnight. From their conversations, Abigail knew that by that point Grandma had made the decision to let her daughter go her own way. She had done her best in raising

Sarah, but Sarah had turned out rotten anyway. Still, losing family was never easy.

"I got to know Granny Lane a bit better later on when..." James stared out the passenger side window. "Well, later on. Dad worked a lot then. At least, he was going into the office a lot. I stayed away from home too, always biking the streets with my friends."

"The mean streets of Wallace Point," Abigail said. "Sounds rough."

James chuckled. "Sometimes it was. This was before the Golf Cart Grannies were a thing."

"I call them the Granny Gang."

"Even better. But without them roaming the streets, we got ourselves into whatever trouble we could rustle up. Nothing too terrible, but nothing promising either. People didn't know what to do with me. They left it up to my dad, but he was too busy trying to keep his own head above water.

"Granny Lane knew I needed guidance, so she asked me to come and help her at the store a few days a week after school. She made me watch these old black and white movies. She said I needed to make sure the films were intact all the way through, but I think she had other intentions."

"She's sneaky like that."

"Those movies were nothing like the stuff coming out in theaters then. My favorites were the noirs. The femmes fatales, the trench coats, the way a good detective always caught his man. I ate it up, along with heaps of cookies."

He shifted in the seat, smiling as he recalled his memories of Grandma. "She never treated me differently, the way everyone else did. She went right on being a smart-mouth with a big heart. It doesn't sound like much, I guess, but it meant a lot to me."

Abigail imagined her grandmother a decade or two younger. Her hair was probably graying at that point, but not yet the halo of white that it was now. She would have had fewer wrinkles, maybe clearer eyes. But she had still been the same woman—wise, loving, and smart.

Abigail was just about to say something nice to James when a sudden snore interrupted her. She looked over at him to see he was fast asleep, his mouth hanging open.

She shook her head in disbelief. "You've got to be kidding me." She sighed and settled into the driver's seat for the long drive.

ABIGAIL CALLED Grandma as they approached an abandoned gas station along a deserted country road. "We're here," she said. "Start the clock."

James sat up in his seat, creased and rumpled after his long nap, but fully alert. There was another car already in the empty lot when they pulled in. Abigail didn't know too much about cars, but it was obvious this vehicle was a modified Japanese import—the kind of car one could hear coming a mile away. It had black tinted windows, keeping its driver a mystery.

Abigail parked her car but left it running. James grabbed the duffel bag he'd tossed into the backseat and the two stepped out into the wind and drizzle.

The door to the other car opened and a man stepped out. Abigail immediately felt there was something familiar about him. He wore a black trench coat, black pants, and a black beanie.

A split second later, Abigail realized who the collector reminded her of: Mary's description of the killer caught on tape.

CHAPTER ELEVEN

Rain flew into Abigail's eyes as she and James edged toward the man dressed in black. Gusts of wind howled around them, drowning out the sound of their running engines. Time felt as if it had slowed. Abigail wondered whether James had seen the motel tapes, or if he had spoken with Mary. Did he have any inkling of the danger they might be in?

Keeping an eye on the man in black, Abigail watched James approach the stranger. He moved cautiously, but he didn't show any signs of fear.

The man in black came closer. "What's in the bag?" His voice was hoarse and shaky. That caught Abigail off guard. Was this guy actually afraid? Or was this some type of tactic?

James unzipped the bag, keeping his gaze trained on the stranger. He pulled out a ragged shirt, shook it out so the man could see the rips in the fabric and the splatters of blood, and then he stuffed it back in the bag.

The shirt belonged to James. Or, it had belonged to him, before Abigail had taken a pair of shears to it. Grandma had dyed the corn syrup herself. She managed to create a shade that looked disturbingly like old, dried blood.

Enticed by the glimpse of the shirt, the stranger stepped closer and Abigail was finally able to get a good look at him.

The guy was hardly more than a kid—a tall kid, maybe, but a kid nonetheless. He was skinny and pale. A fine stubble grew on his gaunt cheeks. Dark bags wallowed under eyes sunken into an angular, sallow face.

Abigail got the feeling this guy spent most of his time in front of a computer screen.

"Let me see it again," the collector said. His voice cracked.

James grinned. "No. Change of plans."

The collector's eyes flicked back and forth between James, Abigail, and the bag. "I don't like this. Your girlfriend already changed the plans once."

Abigail inwardly flinched, but she kept her face free of any emotions. For now, all she could do was hope James was somehow too focused on the situation to notice the 'girlfriend' bit.

"Yeah, well, I hear you have the original murder weapon." James took another step toward the collector. "I'm willing to pay a lot for it."

The collector shifted his slight weight from one combat

booted foot to the next. "I don't know what you're talking about."

"I think you do," Abigail said. She had been the one to contact the kid, so she hoped he might still have a smidgen of trust in her. "I asked around. A couple of sources said you had the same weapon used by the Wallace Point Ripper. We've got money."

The collector smirked. "Your sources lied. Who were they, by the way? I'll have to remember to set them straight."

Suddenly, James took two quick strides and closed the gap between him and the collector. The collector was tall, but James was taller and broader. "You know I won't tell you that. So how about it?"

The collector took a step back, his back smacking against the side of his car. "Look, we have no business here. You want to buy what I can't sell. I want to buy what you won't sell. Guess we should just go our separate ways."

James slammed his hands on both sides of the collector, blocking him in. "You're not going anywhere until you sell us that knife."

The collector's pale face somehow became paler. "Okay, okay, fine. I used to have the knife, all right? But I don't anymore. I sold it."

James growled, "Who bought it?"

The collector put his hands up to keep James from coming any closer to his face. "I have to protect my buyers. I'm sure you understand."

James snapped. He grabbed the collector roughly by

the collar and shook him. "Listen, punk. We've been nice up until now, but you're really testing my patience. A piece of your collection was used in a murder. All I need is a court order to make your life pretty difficult until you talk. And trust me, I can get a court order. I'm sure *you* understand."

"All right, all right!" The collector cleared his throat. "The truth is, I don't know who bought it."

Abigail watched as James's jaw tightened, and for a moment she worried he might get physical with the kid. Well, more physical than he had already gotten.

But, thankfully, the collector seemed to have lost his nerve. "I swear, man, I swear. Whoever it was reached out to me via email. I knew when I saw the email address that it was fishy, so I was pretty wary of doing business with this person. But they made an offer I couldn't refuse, and they were willing to pay half up front before I even dropped off the knife."

"How?"

"How what?"

James gave the collector a hard shake. "How did they make the payment?"

"They sent me the payment through an untraceable digital currency. There's no way to figure out who paid me. Believe me, I tried."

"Okay. Then what?"

"They told me to leave the knife in this old mailbox at an abandoned house in the middle of nowhere. I dropped the knife off just like they told me to, and before I even drove away, I got the other half of the payment."

James's grip tightened on the collar, starting to cut off the guy's circulation. "That's not good enough!"

"Wait!" the guy sputtered. "Wait. I can tell you one more thing, okay? But then you gotta let me go!"

"Fine. What?"

"Whoever it was, they bought the knife a week before the murder. Now seriously, I told you everything."

James released the collector, who fell onto the muddy ground. "There we go. Being helpful wasn't so hard, was it?"

Coughing, the collector scrambled to his feet, jumped into his car, and sped out of the abandoned parking lot.

James turned to Abigail. "What do you say we get out of the rain, Cupcake?"

Abigail wordlessly followed James back to her car. Inside, she pulled out her phone and called Grandma, saying, "Hey, we're done talking to him. Or should I say, *interrogating* him." She gave James a sideways look. "Anyway, we're gonna drive back now. I'll tell you the details later. Okay, see you." When she hung up the phone, James was grinning at her.

"What?"

"So, 'girlfriend,' huh?"

Abigail put the car in drive. "So, 'court order,' huh? Since when do you have that kind of authority?"

"Well, my father can get a court order. But it's not exactly intimidating to say, 'I'm gonna tell my dad on you.'"

"Mmmhmm."

James laughed before looking off in thought. "So, we didn't get a name, but we did get some helpful information."

"You mean when you shook that poor kid by his collar? What did he give us?"

"Whoever bought the knife is tech savvy. How many people know the ins and outs of digital currency?"

"That's a good point," Abigail admitted. "That could narrow down our list of suspects. Right. So, somebody who's tech savvy..."

"That rules out your grandmother, at least."

Abigail laughed, then stopped herself, putting on a glare instead. She didn't want to let James off the hook that easily. "Still, I don't think you had to shake that poor kid up."

James shrugged and crossed his arms, leaning back. "Eh, can't fault me for having a few unresolved anger issues." With that, he resumed his nap from earlier.

Abigail shook her head in disbelief before starting the long drive back home.

CHAPTER TWELVE

When Abigail and James pulled back into the parking lot of the antique store, Thor was sitting on the front porch. He bounded toward them as they stretched, stiff from so much time in the cramped car.

Thor sniffed Abigail's hand before noticing James. He immediately gave the man a slobbery kiss.

"Whoa there, boy!" James said, laughing. He then commented to Abigail, "Your vicious guard dog has really taken to me!"

Abigail mumbled unconvincingly, "He's just... softening you up for when he eats you later." She then stretched her arms to the sky. It felt good to work out the kinks in her back and legs.

The drizzle that had persisted most of the day finally

subsided. Overhead, however, thick, dark clouds continued to churn ominously.

"Looks like more rain tonight," James said.

Missy appeared on the porch, followed closely behind by Grandma. "You're back! Come in! I just set the table for an early dinner."

"I won't say no to a dinner by Granny Lane," James said, and they headed inside.

Rich, savory smells lured them into the kitchen. On the little table, Grandma had set a big bowl of fresh salad, a crusty loaf of sourdough topped with garlic and butter, and a hearty lasagna still steaming from the oven.

James's stomach growled loud enough for Grandma and Abigail to hear. He grinned sheepishly. "I guess I'm hungrier than I thought."

"Well, sit down and dig in," Grandma said. "There's plenty to go around. But my only condition is that you tell me everything that happened with that collector."

Abigail and James didn't waste any time taking Grandma up on her offer. Between mouthfuls of lasagna and salad, they recalled the past couple of hours.

James proved to have a sharp memory. He was able to describe in detail the collector's clothes, his body language, the features of his face, and his car's make and model. Abigail chimed in to proudly recite the first four numbers off the license plate, only to have James fill in the numbers she had missed. Even Abigail was mildly impressed.

Once they had eaten everything there was to eat and told

everything there was to tell, James pushed his chair away from the table and stood. "Well, ladies, it's time I head back home. Thank you for the company today, Abigail. And thank you for the meal, Granny Lane."

Grandma laughed. It wasn't her normal, throaty cackle. It was higher pitched, closer to a titter than a guffaw, the sort of giggle one would expect from a schoolgirl. Abigail arched an eyebrow, but Grandma didn't seem to notice. "Don't mention it, James. It's always a pleasure. Let us walk you to the door."

"No, Granny, you two stay here. I'll see myself out."

"All right, dear. Give your father a hug for me." Grandma smiled as he left the room. She then cocked her head, listening for the sound of his engine. When the parking lot was quiet again, Grandma turned to Abigail. "All right," she said, a gleam in her eyes. "Tell me everything."

Abigail frowned. "What do you mean? I'm pretty sure we covered every detail."

"Yes, but how did you and James get along?"

"Fine, I guess. He was kind of annoying on the road, with all his snoring. And he was pretty scary when we met that guy."

"So, you like him then."

"Yeah, he's nice enough."

Grandma narrowed her eyes, and her lips stuck out into a pout. "But do you *like* him?"

"Grandma, I just said I did."

Grandma huffed and stood up from her seat. She began to clear the table. "Oh, you're not getting it."

Abigail watched her grandmother stack the plates and bowls in the sink before moving on to put away the leftovers in the fridge. Abigail stood, went to the sink, and began to wash the dishes. She was starting to figure out what Grandma was *really* asking. "Do you mean to ask if I like him romantically?"

Grandma paused at the refrigerator and nodded, her lips pressed together.

"Then the answer is no," Abigail said as she scrubbed a casserole dish. "I'm not the romantic type, Grandma. I get the feeling he isn't either." She paused for a moment before adding, "We're both professionals. We're just trying to get to the bottom of this case."

Grandma sighed. "Romance isn't what it used to be." Her voice carried a note of wistfulness. "Two nice young adults with the same interests and the thought doesn't even occur to them. Back when I was young, that kind of thing was worth celebrating."

"Jeez, Grandma. Not everything is peachy with him. You didn't see what I saw today."

"What do you mean?"

Abigail poked at her lip. She recalled the way James had grabbed the collector's collar and had gotten right up into his face. When she had caught a glimpse of James's eyes, she saw a lot of anger. But did she want to tell Grandma that? She decided against it. "I don't know.

It's just, he's been in New Jersey for ten years now, right?"

"Yes."

"That's plenty of time for a person to change. And with such a traumatic childhood..." Abigail trailed off. She waited for Grandma to make some comment or objection. When it didn't come, she turned from the sink.

Grandma was sitting at the table. Her usually bright eyes were wet with pent up tears. "I had really hoped he would turn out all right, despite everything."

"Oh, Grandma." Abigail dried her hands and went to hug the old woman. "Forget I said anything. I guess all these murders just have me seeing the worst in people."

"If you say so."

"Not that I'm about to let up on this case. I'm worried about Sheriff Wilson. I know this is all hard for him, and because he has such a difficult history with this case, I'm worried he might have some blind spots. It's those blind spots that I want to look at more closely."

Grandma gave a tiny sniffle and wiped her eyes. "There's a festival happening in a couple of days. On Friday night."

Abigail frowned at the sudden change in subject, but she pondered the upcoming holidays. She couldn't think of any that would warrant a festival. "Okay. What's the festival for?"

"It's 'The Last Hurrah.' It's the last little celebration the town throws before tourist season starts up again."

Abigail gasped. "With all the excitement the past couple of days, I'd totally forgotten about the incoming tourists."

Grandma nodded matter-of-factly. "Yes. With winter almost here, we're about to lose the town to tourists for a little while. Wallace Point is quite the Christmastime destination, you know. So pretty much every local shows up at this festival for one final hurrah."

Abigail nodded, her face lighting up. "I see! It's the perfect time to sniff out potential suspects, right?"

"Goodness, no. I was hoping it would get your mind *off* the investigation."

"Good luck with that," Abigail said with a small snicker. "Anyway, why are you so hot and cold about this investigation? You were all for uncovering Reginald Grimes's murderer."

"That was different. I just hate this whole Wallace Point Ripper mess. I wish it would just go away."

"Figuring out who did it is the only way we can make this go away permanently."

Grandma sighed. "I suppose you're right."

"Of course I'm right," Abigail said with a mischievous grin. She went back to the sink full of dishes and began to scrub in earnest. The festival would be a great place to sniff out some clues.

With any luck, James would be there so she could keep an eye on him. And with any *more* luck, she might even stumble across a tech savvy culprit.

CHAPTER THIRTEEN

When Friday rolled around, the storm clouds had moved on and a determined cold had settled in. Abigail sat with Thor on the front porch steps. He had his big head nestled in her lap while she pulled on his floppy ears.

Their usually sleepy neighborhood was quite alive this afternoon. All of Wallace Point seemed to be looking forward to The Last Hurrah before gearing up for the holiday tourist season.

Moms, dads, kids, and grandparents trickled out of their homes and onto the sidewalks on their way to the festival. They were all bundled against the cold, smiling up into the clear blue sky overhead, breathing in the crisp air of autumn by the sea.

Abigail had dressed warmly too. She wore black fleece-lined leggings, an oversized cable knit white sweater that almost reached her knees, her favorite scarf, and flat-heeled black boots. On her head she wore a thick wool cap, and on her hands she wore gray mittens. She felt warm and happy and ready to do a bit of investigating.

"Hello there."

Abigail looked up from Thor's sleepy tan face. Camille Bellerose stood on the sidewalk, smiling at her and Thor. A little breeze teased Camille's hair, and with her tall, thin, graceful shape, she looked like a sapling tree swaying in the wind. Abigail imagined that if such things as nymphs existed, Camille was certainly one of them.

"Hello, Camille," Abigail called back. "On your way to the festival?"

"Of course! I wouldn't miss the last bit of fun before the tourists come. Are you coming to the festival?"

"Yep. Just waiting on Grandma."

Right on cue, Grandma stepped out onto the porch with Missy at her heels. She sported loose, well-worn jeans, a chunky sweater festooned with red, orange, and gold leaf appliqué, and a thick hand-knit scarf wrapped securely over her chest and neck.

Despite her festive outfit, however, Grandma's face wore a rare look: a scowl.

She looked so adorable that Abigail laughed out loud.

"We were just chatting about you, Granny Lane," Camille said.

Abigail nodded. "I was telling her how long you take to powder your nose."

Grandma sniffed and set her hands on her hips. "My nose hasn't seen powder in a decade. Now behave, Camille, or I'll ban you from the store."

"Ban me?"

"It's a brilliant concept Abigail came up with. If I'm upset with someone, or if I suspect them of anything at all, then I simply ban them from the store."

"But Granny Lane," Camille said, her narrow face crestfallen. "I didn't even say anything. It was all Abigail. And she didn't say anything either, come to think of it."

"It's the company you keep, Camille. Besides, I haven't gotten to ban anyone yet, and I can't very well ban my granddaughter from her own home now, can I?"

Abigail stood. "You'll have to excuse her, Camille. Grandma's grumpy because she's missing her afternoon nap on account of The Last Hurrah."

"I'm not grumpy," Grandma grumbled. "I just think Wallace Point should be more considerate of regular nap hours."

Camille butted in, "Don't worry, Granny Lane. I know what will perk you right up."

"What's that, Camille?"

"For once, you don't have to make the sweets! Everyone else is making all sorts of treats just for you. All you have to do is walk downtown and fill your plate!"

Grandma's face transformed from dark and brooding to

bright and eager. "You make an excellent point! They're sure to have pies and cakes. Oh, do you think there will be cinnamon rolls again this year?"

Camille shook her head and laughed. "Let's go and find out."

THE WALK to downtown Wallace Point was a short and sweet one. The sound of folk music grew louder and louder as they drew closer. Soon, the clusters of pedestrians merged into the small crowds that ambled around stalls and booths.

There were vendors selling jewelry, art, books, and plants. Grandma and Abigail lost Camille to a man dressed in overalls who promised the biggest blueberries Wallace Point had ever seen.

Grandma wasn't interested in any of that. "Follow your nose," she advised Abigail. "Your nose will never lead you astray."

"I'm pretty sure you're addicted to sugar, Grandma," Abigail said. Then she noticed a pair of uniformed police officers strolling down the sidewalk. Despite the gaiety surrounding them, the officers looked quite serious.

Why were there police officers at The Last Hurrah? Were they searching for suspects too?

"Oh, look Abigail. It's Sheriff Wilson and James."

Abigail looked in the direction Grandma gestured and spotted the father and son duo walking down the sidewalk on the other side of the street. Sheriff Wilson was dressed in his uniform, though James had on his usual rumpled attire and trench coat.

It was the first time in days that Abigail had caught a glimpse of the sheriff, and she didn't like what she saw. The man looked worn out, his skin pallid and puffy. Taking each step seemed to cost him, and yet he kept moving forward. James walked at his side, his own face impassive.

"Should we go say hi, Grandma?"

For a long moment, Grandma paused in her pursuit of sugar and regarded James and Sheriff Wilson. Finally she shook her head. "Let's not. I think Willy has enough on his mind at the moment."

Abigail nodded her acceptance. "Let's walk a little more then. I think I see some bedazzled golf carts."

Sure enough, just a block or two down, the Granny Gang was hawking sock monkeys.

"Monkeys! Get your monkeys here!" crowed one granny. Her golf cart was painted a metallic gold with red flames.

Another golf cart was a candy apple red. It had racing stripes painted down its little front hood. "Get 'em while you still can!" this granny squawked. "Get 'em before the tourists do!"

"Hey little lady." A granny dressed in an oversized pea coat slid in front of Abigail and blocked her path. Behind her was an exceptionally fancy ride. The front and rear of the golf cart was shaped like an antique Bel Air.

But Abigail didn't get to study the vehicle for long. The

granny before her hadn't finished her spiel. "You look stressed, nervous, uptight. You look like you need..." The granny stopped to cast a few suspicious looks around her. Then, she opened her pea coat with a flourish. "A sock monkey!"

Dangling from the inside panels of the pea coat were all types of sock monkeys. Some of them were made of white socks or brown socks. Some were different species, like lions and elephants. Others had long purple hair or short red curls. One sock monkey even sported a pair of spectacles.

"Doreen!" Grandma cackled. "You've outdone yourself!"

Doreen curtsied, still holding her pea coat open. "Thank you, thank you! Why aren't you here with us, Florence?"

"Oh, I don't know how all of you are doing it without your regular nap. This time of day is when I take a little power nap."

"It does get tougher every year." Doreen sighed. "I just took an early morning nap, drank a pot of green tea, and that sent me right off."

"Green tea, huh? I need to get me some of that."

Doreen's focus shifted to people behind them. "Florence, I'd love to stay and chat, but I just spotted a bulging wallet and a sullen little cherub. The socks must be sold!" With that, Doreen dashed off as fast as a granny dressed in an oversized pea coat weighed down with a dozen sock monkeys could dash.

Abigail shivered. "Ruthless."

"My nose! Abigail, my nose tells me there are warm

drinks and sweets this way. Let's go!" Grandma grabbed Abigail by the elbow and dragged her along with a shocking amount of strength.

They came upon the coffee and tea first. Bobby and Sally Kent manned a rolling drink cart. The cart had two large wheels, similar to bicycle wheels on one end of the cart body. On the other end were two small wheels, like the wheels on a grocery cart. A little black and white awning stretched over the whole contraption.

"Abigail!" Sally said when she caught sight of them. "And Granny Lane!" She ran over and gave them both a quick hug. "You ladies look lovely as always."

"Look what we've got here! The Lanes!" Bobby announced grandly to no one in particular. An almost foolish but totally genuine smile stretched across his face. "What sights for sore eyes!"

"Sally, Bobby! How's the coffee selling?"

"Like hotcakes." Bobby grinned. "The Mad Brothers just bought a liter each!"

Abigail frowned. "The Mad Brothers?"

Sally explained, "He means the Madsens. You know, Kirby and Dag." Sally's bright blue eyes took on an extra shine when she muttered Dag's name. "They were just here. He's not kidding about the liter of coffee. They're lugging these enormous mugs around, and they stopped here to fill up." Sally leaned close to Abigail and whispered, "It was the funniest thing. Dag and I were catching up, so Dad tried his best to make small talk with Kirby. You should have seen Kirby's face! Poor guy looked miserable."

Abigail smothered a laugh as she imagined the ever-dire Kirby standing next to Bobby, the town's game show host. "I'm not surprised. Kirby isn't the small talk type."

Grandma tugged on Abigail's arm. "We're close," she said, sniffing the air. "We're really close."

Sally looked at Abigail, who shook her head. "Grandma's got a serious craving for sugar. She missed her nap."

"Ah." Sally nodded meaningfully. "Well, I'll fix you right up with a cup of coffee for you and a cup of tea for Granny, and then we'll send you on your way."

Grandma found the sweets soon enough. Booths, food trucks, and stalls were all selling fresh fried donuts, pies, and funnel cakes. Then there were heaps and heaps of cookies and homemade chocolates. And, of course, there were cobblers and cakes. Anything Grandma could want was waiting for her.

Unfortunately, Grandma wanted everything. After she'd bought a funnel cake, a slice of apple pie, and double choco-late cookies, Abigail saw that she had better remove Grandma from temptation before the woman put herself in a sugar coma. That was when she spotted the lighthouse.

"Hey Grandma," Abigail said, gently steering her grand-mother away from the dessert vendors. "Why don't we visit Lee?"

"In the lighthouse?" Grandma asked around a mouthful of pie.

"Sure. We haven't seen him in so long."

"Not yet. I just found the cinnamon roll booth."

"But Grandma, you don't have any room on your plate."

Grandma looked down and saw that Abigail was right. One more sweet crumb and her pile of food would topple over. "Oh, all right."

Abigail led her grandmother down the road to the lighthouse. Thus far, she hadn't noticed anyone acting suspiciously, but the festival was far from over. Something important was bound to happen sooner or later. Abigail was sure of it.

CHAPTER FOURTEEN

The walk to the lighthouse was an uphill one, but along the way Abigail and Grandma managed to pick up Camille again. She carried a heavy potted plant under her arm and a satisfied smile on her face. The sun started to set as the three of them arrived at the lighthouse garden gate.

Grandma had finished her treats on the walk and was now licking the sugar off her fingers. She heaved a contented, slightly out of breath sigh. "What absolutely divine baked goods."

Lee Lebeau was working in his garden with his back to the gate, unaware of their approach until Grandma spoke. Then he half-jumped, half-turned, and fully tripped over his own long legs. He eventually succeeded in unraveling his lengthy limbs and limped over to open the gate.

"Hello," he said. He unlatched the gate with one hand and

rubbed a sore spot on his hip with the other. "What a nice surprise."

"Hello dear," Grandma greeted cheerfully. She was finally back to her usual granny self after her sugar feast. "We were in the area for the festival and thought we'd pop over to say hello."

"Oh, that's right. The Last Hurrah is tonight, isn't it?"

"No," Abigail shook her head. "It isn't tonight. It's right now. You didn't see or hear all the commotion just down the hill?"

Lee gave them a rueful smile. "I guess not. I've been so busy fixing up this garden and old lighthouse that I've completely lost track of my days." He glanced over at Camille curiously.

Abigail said, "You do know Camille, don't you?"

He shook his head, as did Camille. "I'm Lee Lebeau," he said, holding his hand out for her to shake.

Camille shook his scrawny hand, paying no heed to the dirt. "Camille. I'm a teacher down at the elementary school."

"Oh. I used to work at the marina. Maybe that's why we've never run into each other."

"The garden is coming together," Camille observed. She cast a practiced eye over the little plot of land. "I remember back when this place was abandoned. I thought it was a shame for this land to be so overgrown. Are you going with an English cottage garden plan?"

"Yes, actually. I'm going to fill this place with as many sweet-smelling flowers as it can hold. I'm also thinking about putting in a little patch for vegetables, maybe a few fruit trees."

"Have you considered a beehive?"

"Of course. I would also like small livestock. You know, chickens, maybe a goat, but I'm not sure the city will go for it."

Abigail looked from one garden enthusiast to the other and nearly groaned. She liked trees and flowers of course. Bushes were all right if they had edible berries. But she'd never had the patience for gardening, and she couldn't understand dedicating hours of one's life to digging in the dirt.

Then again, better to dig in the dirt than run around murdering people.

A low and rumbling *mrrreow* made the three of them jump as Lee's three-legged cat hobbled on past them.

Camille knelt to scratch the black and white cat's ear. "What a funny little meow you have, kitty."

"That's Blackbeard," Lee said, brushing some dirt off his hands. "That cat's more pirate than me, despite my family's lineage."

"Oh. You'll have to tell me about that sometime," Camille replied, twirling her hair. Abigail almost laughed at how obvious the flirtation was. She couldn't deny that the two would make a pretty cute couple, though...

"So, Lee," Grandma began. "How is the inside of the light-house coming along?"

Lee's face brightened. "Oh, quite well, actually. Would

you like to see it? Camille, let's just put your plant here by the door. That way you won't have to lug it around."

"You don't think anyone will take it, do you? I had to haggle for a full fifteen minutes for this baby."

"Oh, it'll be fine. After all, the tourists aren't here yet."

Lee held his hands out for the plant, unprepared for its weight. When he almost dropped it, Camille snatched it back from him.

"Err, I can carry it to the door, Lee, but thanks for trying."

"Right," he said, failing to hide his embarrassment as he rubbed his arm. "Okay, this way then." Lee tugged on the heavy wooden door of the lighthouse and stepped inside. The space was round, with flagstone floors and walls that were white in some places, but mostly yellow and cracked with age. "This is the first floor. Essentially a sitting room or parlor. I haven't had many visitors yet, so I haven't gotten around to it."

A narrow spiral staircase on their left curved upwards through a hole in the ceiling. They took this staircase and found themselves in a small rounded kitchen, complete with a wood burning stove, a wooden table with two chairs, and a host of pots and pans.

"This is the kitchen," Lee announced awkwardly.

"Why, Lee, I never would have guessed," Grandma said with a teasing twinkle in her eye. "Did you have to do much to it?"

"Quite a bit. It's taken some elbow grease, but it's about ready now."

Abigail waved toward the cast iron stove. It looked like something from a Victorian romance movie. "Do you cook on this quaint little thing?"

"Not yet. But that stove will get good and hot once it's lit. It just hasn't been cold enough to fire her up yet."

The next rounded floor was a bedroom with a tiny attached bathroom. Aside from the bed, a desk with a chair, and a dresser, there wasn't room for much else. But the place was snug and clean enough to make it cozy.

The final leg of the spiral staircase brought them to the light room. "It's automated now," Lee explained. "Well, it used to be automated. This lighthouse has been neglected for a while. I'm in the process of fixing what I can. For the rest, I'll phone an expert when it's time."

"I must say, I'm very impressed," Grandma said. "You've done a lot in a short amount of time."

"Well, I had plenty of anger at the beginning to put a fire in my belly. You know, with all the stuff my dad put me through."

Abigail could understand that, considering what had happened to him a few months ago. The group was just about to head back down when the sound of angry voices floated up the hill and through the open windows of the lighthouse. Like good Wallace Point residents, they crept to the windows to see the commotion.

Down at the bottom of the hill, James and Rachel Cuthbert were having words. The wind that had carried the tone of their argument up to the lighthouse was now toying with the arguers. Her hair kept flying into her eyes. His trench coat kept flapping around him like wings.

Their voices grew louder and louder, but no more distinct. Finally, Rachel stormed off in a huff, leaving James pacing and still shouting.

"I wonder what that was all about?" Camille asked, breaking the silence.

Abigail was wondering the same thing. She hadn't seen Rachel since that night at the bowling alley. What could she and James possibly be fighting about? Abigail wasn't sure, but she was rearing to find out. "Camille," she said. "Maybe we should go check on your plant."

Camille's face went pale. "You don't think..."

Abigail only shrugged.

In no time, the group was standing by the front door, where Camille's plant contentedly soaked up the final rays of the setting sun. That was when Camille caught sight of a rosebush crawling up one side of the lighthouse. "Lee," she said, her hand reaching out to clutch his sleeve. "Is that a David Austin rose?"

Lee broke into a wide grin and puffed out his chest. "Yes, yes, it is."

Abigail and Grandma shared a look. "You thinking what I'm thinking?" Abigail whispered.

Grandma blinked. "Am I?"

"I'm thinking we should talk to that reporter."

"Oh. I was thinking how nice one of those cinnamon rolls would be right about now."

Abigail laughed. "Cinnamon rolls later. Reporter now."

"But Abigail, what if they sell out?"

"Then you'll avoid acquiring diabetes in the span of one evening."

"Oh, fine." Grandma stifled a cackle. "I'll admit, I too am a little curious about why they were arguing."

Abigail whirled around to face Lee and Camille. "Hey Camille, I think we're heading back now. You want to come?"

Camille's nose was buried deep in the last rose on the rosebush. Her face was dreamy when she responded, "That's all right. I'm just going to stop and smell the roses a bit longer."

Abigail didn't wait for her to change her mind. She grabbed Grandma's elbow and guided her down the road back toward the festival. She hoped they wouldn't be too late to catch Rachel Cuthbert.

CHAPTER FIFTEEN

With the setting of the sun, the festival was now in full swing. The streets of downtown Wallace Point were more crowded than they had ever been since Abigail first visited. Children ran from one dessert vendor to the next while their parents, clustered together, watched and longed for the energy of youth. Teenagers sauntered about in pairs, if they were lucky enough to have dates, or in groups that, out of sheer jealousy, mocked the couples.

Rachel Cuthbert had disappeared into the crowd, and Abigail was starting to worry she wouldn't find her. Luckily, after checking with the Granny Gang, Grandma tracked her down at the local toy store.

The store was closed for the festival, but the window display, illuminated by twinkling lights, had drawn a crowd of children. To Abigail's surprise, the toys in the display were dancing.

A limber ballerina spun on her toe, while, beside her, a wooden old couple did a jittery jig. In a corner, a group of toy schoolchildren the size of Abigail's pinky swayed on a tiny wooden stage. Above them all, a trapeze artist swung up, over, and around a tightrope.

Mr. Yamamoto's toy store wasn't the run of the mill collection of molded plastic in primary colors. He built many of the intricate toys himself out of wood, and sold a wide array of board games on top of that.

Abigail hadn't explored the store yet because she was certain she'd break every one of Mr. Yamamoto's delicate creations. But every time she had walked by in the past, she would always bring her face close to the glass and admire the breathtaking displays.

Tonight though, she wasn't focused on the window.

Rachel Cuthbert crouched at a corner of the display. She wore all black, and in her hands she carried a heavy camera with an impressive lens. While the children ogled the moving toys, Rachel snapped photo after photo of their entranced faces.

Abigail and Grandma walked up behind her. At first, they waited politely for her to finish her photography. But when she continued to take shot after shot after shot, Abigail lost her patience.

"Hey Rachel!" she said brightly.

Rachel jerked, nearly dropping her camera. She had such

a stricken look on her face that Abigail wondered if Rachel had expected to find the Ripper behind her with a knife. Grandma struggled to suppress a snicker.

"You scared the daylights out of me!" Rachel exclaimed. She didn't seem to find the incident as humorous as Grandma did. "What do you want?"

Abigail, sensing that Rachel wasn't in a talkative mood, tried to ease into the conversation.

"We just saw you snapping pictures," she lied. "We thought we'd say hello."

Rachel's face softened slightly. "Well, hey. Hi, Mrs. Lane."

"Hello, Rachel." Grandma nodded at the bulky camera. "Are you working for the paper again?"

"Yeah, they're letting me cover The Last Hurrah. It's no one's dream job, but the paper has me on probation."

"A job's a job, Rachel. You'll have the town's confidence again soon enough."

"Maybe. I'm not sure about a few people though."

Abigail saw her chance. "Do you mean James? I saw you two arguing earlier."

Rachel groaned. "Yup. That guy is a total hot head."

"James?" Grandma crooned, letting her voice tremble just a bit. "Why, I always thought he was such a sweetheart. What happened?"

"I don't really know. One minute I was taking photos, the next he was blocking my view. He kept going on about the Wallace Point Ripper. He warned me to stop pursuing that angle."

Abigail frowned. "Pursuing it? Why would he think you're still pursuing it?"

"Probably because I still am. Look, I issued that apology in the newspaper and I meant it. I shouldn't have published what I did without stronger evidence. But there are details I just can't get over. I guess I still have my suspicions."

"But why would dear, sweet James threaten you over that?" Grandma pursued.

"No idea." Rachel looked down at her camera and played around with its settings for a moment. "It just doesn't make any sense. You'd think he would want more coverage of the killer who slaughtered his mother. How else will the guy get caught?"

"Maybe James doesn't want to relive the past," Abigail suggested.

"Then he should stop snooping around in my business. I understand it must be painful for him. I get that. I really do. But the killer's still out there. The story is still relevant, and to more people than just himself."

Rachel didn't sound the least bit sympathetic toward James's pain. When she said the story was still relevant, Abigail could have sworn she heard her say that the story was still profitable.

"Well, I'm sorry you had to go through that, dear," Grandma was saying. "I'm sure he'll come around eventually."

Rachel shrugged. "He can do whatever he wants as long as he stays out of my way. Anyhow, I've got to keep working.

See you later." Without waiting for Grandma and Abigail to respond, Rachel disappeared into the crowd.

Grandma pouted. "That girl is just as rude as when she was a teenager."

"I guess Mom always had a knack for finding shady friends."

Grandma had a faraway look in her eyes. "Not always." She shook her head. "Anyway, I can understand why James would have a problem with Rachel. Rachel is just out for a buck."

"I don't know, Grandma. It makes sense that he doesn't like Rachel. I don't like her much myself. But don't you think his interaction with her was a tad too aggressive?"

Grandma sighed. She turned to face a new set of kids who currently had their noses pressed up against the toy store window. After studying their expressions for a minute, she nodded. "James threatening anyone does seem out of character. We should let him defend himself."

"Do you think he'll volunteer that kind of information?"

"No, we'll have to pull it out of him. Get him to lower his guard before he starts spilling."

"You could bake him some cookies."

"Too obvious." Grandma shook her head. "You could ask him out on a date."

"Grandma! No way. We've talked about this."

"All right, all right, keep your hose on. It was just a suggestion. Wait! I've got it! In the morning, we'll give him a call and ask him to come over to the store. We can tell him we have an antique that he'd love. Then once we have him buttered up, that's when we ask him about the reporter."

Abigail grinned. "That's more like it. Much better than me going out on a date with him." She pretended to gag.

"Oh, hush with that. I'm just trying to be helpful. Anyways, we've gone to the lighthouse to see Lee. We tracked Rachel down and picked her brain. And we've come up with a plan to ensnare James. Now can we *please* go get some cinnamon rolls?"

"Okay, Grandma. But only if you promise me that you're done with sugar tonight after the rolls. You're starting to worry me."

Grandma narrowed her eyes at Abigail, but Abigail held her ground. She figured it was only a matter of time before Grandma's sugar high turned into a sugar low. Hopefully a cinnamon roll would provide just the right amount of energy to get her home.

"Fine," Grandma finally grumbled. "You'd think at my age I'd get to have a bit of fun."

CHAPTER SIXTEEN

The next morning, Abigail went on her morning run with Thor. The cold stung her cheeks and numbed her hands. Although the sun shone bright in the clear sky, it did nothing to warm her up; she had to run faster just to maintain a comfortable body temperature.

"You're lucky I love you so much, Thor, otherwise I would have just slept in," she wheezed. Thor shot her a grin. His tongue lolled out of one side of his mouth, and his eyes showed just enough white around the irises to make him look crazed.

Grandma wasn't anywhere to be found downstairs when Abigail came through the house, so she trotted up to the old woman's room and knocked on the door.

"Humph!" came the reply.

"Grandma! We've got work to do!"

"I can't get out of bed."

"What?" Panic flashed through Abigail's chest. "Why? What's wrong?"

"I've got a stomach ache from all that sugar last night. Come on in and gloat if you must."

Abigail opened the door and saw that the bed was a pile of tangled blankets. Somewhere underneath that mountain of chenille and flannel was Grandma, curled up into an aching ball.

"I won't gloat. Much. Aren't you happy I didn't let you have that third cinnamon roll?"

"I'm not happy about anything just now. I feel like Humpty Dumpty when he fell off the wall."

Abigail laughed. "My poor, sweet grandma. What can I do to make you feel all better?"

The pile of blankets bulged and swelled, like earth shifting over a burrowing animal. White hair and bright eyes emerged from the cloth cocoon. "A bath?"

"Okay. I'll run you a hot bath then."

"And some tea?"

"Fresh tea coming right up."

Grandma sighed and wriggled the rest of her body out from underneath the blankets. "Thanks, dear. Your little old granny just needs a bit of babying this morning."

"No problem." Abigail went to Grandma's bathroom and started the hot water in the antique claw foot tub. She sprinkled a small handful of lavender Epsom salt in the water to add a soothing fragrance, and she lit a couple of small pillar candles for ambiance. Then she kissed her pouty grand-mother on the forehead before heading downstairs.

Before long, the tea kettle was whistling as Grandma floated down the stairs. "That hot bath was just the thing!" she exclaimed as she waltzed into the kitchen. "I feel all put together again."

"I'm glad to hear it." Abigail poured them both a cup of the steaming liquid.

Grandma grabbed her cup, filled it with milk but skipped the sugar, and made her way into the store. "Let's see," she said, walking in and around her collection of antique odds and ends. "If I were James, what would I want?"

"To catch a killer."

"I can't sell him that."

"To star in a black and white detective movie."

"I can't sell him that either. Now, if you aren't going to be helpful, go stand by the counter."

Abigail did as she was told. She had no desire to shop for James Wilson. After a few minutes, Grandma joined her empty-handed.

"This is a lot harder than I thought." Grandma leaned on the counter and propped her cheek on her hand. "Usually I can find the perfect little knickknack to entice someone to come over when I need them to, but I'm at a loss for what James might like."

"Maybe the guy has no interests."

"Of course he has interests. He's just very discreet. Too discreet for a town like this. That's probably why he moved away, come to think of it. Did he mention any of his interests to you on the drive to meet the collector?"

"Not really. On the way up, he talked about you a little, but then he fell asleep. And again, on the way back, we talked about the case before he fell asleep. Maybe you could give him a pillow?"

"Oh, you're killing me, Abigail. Listen, to sell antiques successfully, you have to figure out what every person's catnip is."

"Catnip?"

"That thing they can't get enough of. Some people like classic cars, Russian novels, unicorns—anything unique to the individual. And once you've learned what someone's catnip is, you can use it as bait."

Abigail thought for a minute. "Like when I knew Sally liked coffee, so I convinced Bobby Kent to buy that wall-mounted grinder for her?"

"Exactly like that!"

Abigail thought some more. "Grandma, what's *my* catnip?"

"Easy," Grandma said absently. Her thoughts were still on James. "A good mystery, book or otherwise. A cozy blanket. A dusty photo album."

Abigail thought a little more before suddenly straightening up. "Hey, wait! So all those times we sat together by the fireplace, you were taking advantage of my catnip? You were getting me exactly where you wanted me—"

"Oh!" Grandma interrupted. "I've just thought of something. I've got this compact antique monocular. Wouldn't that be useful for a private investigator?"

"I guess," Abigail said sullenly. Grandma had conveniently changed the subject and apparently had no intention of going back to it.

"I'll call him right away." Grandma picked up the phone, while Abigail sulked, only to catch herself longing for the embrace of a warm blanket.

THE MONOCULAR WAS MADE of polished brass. It looked like a metal flask, only instead of a round mouth, it had an eyepiece. The lens itself remained hidden inside until the body was opened up like a clam. Then the lens moved from a flat, horizontal position to a vertical one that magnified faraway objects.

"Wow, Granny Lane," James said as he peered through the eyepiece. "You want me to have this?"

"Of course, dear! How long has it been since you had anything from my store? Cookies don't count."

James ran a hand through his disheveled hair. As always, he wore a trench coat over pants and a shirt that desperately needed pressing. "I don't know. I guess it must have been before I moved to the city."

"Well, now you're back. And if you run off again, I want you to have something to remember me by."

"Thanks, Granny Lane. This thing will definitely come in handy."

"Don't mention it. Now, I want you to be straight with me. Has that reporter been harassing you? I'll give her a stern talking to if she is!"

"Erm." James cast a searching look at Abigail. She didn't let her face betray a thing. "Well, I've never liked journalist types, but nobody's been harassing me."

Abigail and Grandma caught each other's eyes. Was he avoiding the subject? Abigail decided to find out. "We ask because last night, during the festival, Grandma and I were visiting the lighthouse. While we were inside, we could hear you and Rachel having a bit of a disagreement."

"To put it kindly," added Grandma.

"Oh, that." James sighed. "She's obsessed with the Ripper. She was asking me things I just didn't want to talk about. Not to her, not to anyone."

Uh oh. This was the complete opposite of what Rachel had told them the night before. She claimed he had approached her, not the other way around. Who was making what up? Abigail kept pushing. "What's her deal anyway?"

"Her piece about the return of the Wallace Point Ripper sold a lot of papers. I mean *a lot*. Even people out of town bought it. I think she's been chasing that high ever since. The problem is, there hasn't been any more big breaks in the story, so she's just been digging and digging, doing anything she can to make a new story happen." James shook his head, and, for once, Abigail caught a flicker of pain in his eyes. "It's just grotesque. She's making a career out of glorifying my mother's killer."

Abigail's stomach turned. The grief James displayed seemed genuine. And it made sense to her why he would have lost his temper with Rachel the night before.

His version of events made more sense than Rachel's. Abigail could easily see Rachel asking a few too many crude questions. She could also see James reacting as dramatically as he had.

But that would mean Rachel lied, which could only mean one thing: Rachel was hiding something.

CHAPTER SEVENTEEN

Rachel was on Abigail's mind the next day as she walked downtown. It was a breezy Sunday, and both Abigail and Grandma were determined to enjoy their day off.

Earlier that morning, Grandma made plans with the Granny Gang, while Abigail made plans to hang out with Sally and Dag. A little while before Abigail set out, Grandma peeled out of the parking lot with a toot of her horn, while Missy hung on for dear life in the passenger seat.

Missy was so well bundled against the chill air that the poor dog couldn't move even if she had wanted to. As they left, Missy looked back at Abigail with wide eyes that said, "The things I do for my human."

Now, Thor loped alongside Abigail, his big feet padding quietly on the sidewalk. Frequently he stopped to sniff a patch of grass or a fire hydrant. Every so often, he'd touch his cold wet nose to Abigail's hand and smile contentedly up at her.

Abigail kept wondering what Rachel was trying to hide. What had she hoped to learn from James? Had she discovered something about the case that she didn't want anyone to know about?

"Hey there, frowny face!" Sally Kent's jovial voice broke into her reverie. "What's on your mind?"

Abigail looked up and realized she had made it to the Book Cafe without even noticing. Sally stood in front of the door wearing blue jeans and a light blue sweater that brought out her eyes. Slung over her shoulder was a canvas bag.

"Just something unpleasant, that's all. Are you ready?"

"All set!"

Sally and Abigail walked down to the Lafayette, where Dag was waiting for them on the ship's deck. He wore a bright smile on his tanned face as his baby blue eyes watched Sally bounce up the gangway. Abigail was a little more cautious during her ascent, even though it wasn't the first time she had been on the ship. Thor seemed to pay no heed to the water below in his excitement to sniff all the new odd scents the ship had to offer him.

The ship rocked gently, almost imperceptibly, with the little waves that lapped against it. Above them, the sun shone bright and warm, vainly doing its best to fight back the cold.

The breeze whipped their faces, teasing Sally's ponytail into a billowing mass of gold.

Abigail inhaled the salty air of the sea. When she exhaled, the Lafayette seemed to exhale with her, creaks and groans escaping from its old wooden joints.

"Thanks for letting us do this, Dag," Sally said, grinning at the stout, muscular keeper sporting a ponytail of his own.

"My pleasure, Sally. I patronize the arts every chance I get. Though, it does help that there aren't any tourists about."

"That's kinda surprising," Abigail said. "Considering that not long ago, the Lafayette was the key to a buried treasure."

"We did get a big influx of visitors right up until last week, mostly people within a few hours drive. I expect we'll get a lot more once the Christmas season is in full swing."

Dag followed Abigail as she followed Sally, who was looking for the perfect bit of detail on the ship to sketch. She settled into a spot at the bow where she had a good view of the figurehead. Then she put down her canvas bag and pulled out a sketch pad and a leather pouch of pencils.

The figurehead was a wooden carving of a mermaid. She was bare-chested, stripped even of the customary seashells. Her tail curled up behind her, and she eagerly looked out to sea with sightless eyes.

Abigail frowned. "She's kinda creepy."

"I think she's beautiful," Sally said. "But then again, I've always had a thing for mermaids. Hey, do you know the difference between a mermaid and a siren?"

Abigail sat on the faded wooden floor, its color bleached

by its years at sea. She stretched out onto her back and let the sun warm her bones as Thor flopped down next to her. "Um, aren't they the same thing?"

Sally shook her head, though her eyes didn't stray from her work. "Sirens were what tempted Odysseus on his voyage home. They are half-birds, half-women with ethereal voices who could sing a sailor to his death. Mermaids, on the other hand, are half-fish, half-women. Over time, people confused the two."

"The Norse had a different idea of mermaids," Dag contributed. Standing there, facing the sea, with tendrils of hair dancing in the wind, he looked every bit like his Viking ancestors.

"Selkies?" Sally guessed.

"That's it. Difference was, they were seals, not fish, and they could shed their skin and come to land. A man who found a selkie's skin and hid it would have her as his wife. They would raise children and live happily ever after... unless she found her skin. Then she'd throw it back on, say goodbye to the kids, and go home."

"What if a woman found a male selkie's skin?" Abigail pondered.

"It could happen, but usually it went the other way around. More often, when a woman disappeared at sea, people would say she had gone off to be with her selkie lover."

"Well, that's not very fair," Sally commented.

Dag grinned. "If it makes you feel any better, sailors

feared mermaids for ages. But then they developed another superstition—that nude or half-nude women could calm the sea. So ship captains started using mermaid figureheads, hoping they would bring them home safely."

Abigail tried to imagine what it must have been like, working on the Lafayette back in the ship's prime. She imagined being out in the open ocean, at the mercy of the weather, trying to catch a *whale* of all things. No wonder the poor sailors hoped a half-naked fish woman would help them.

Dag found a comfortable seat amidst some crates and netting that Abigail suspected were purely decorative. He stared dreamily toward the ocean. "So, what did you think of The Last Hurrah, Abigail?"

"I thought it was fun. We visited Lee at the lighthouse. Grandma gorged on sugar. We had a ball."

"Did I see you talking to that reporter?" Dag asked. "What was her name? The one who claimed the Ripper was behind the motel murder."

"You mean Rachel Cuthbert. Yeah, we said hello."

Sally sighed. "I hope she's okay."

Abigail laughed. "Well, it's not like we gave her a black eye or anything. Just asked a few questions."

Sally stopped sketching and turned to Abigail. "You didn't hear the news?"

Abigail sat up. "Uh. What news?"

"She went missing late last night. I thought you knew. It was in the paper this morning."

"I guess I forgot to look at it. What happened?"

"No one really knows," Dag said. "The door to her apartment was open. Her place was a mess. Apparently one of the other reporters from the paper discovered it after she had failed to send in the photos she took at The Last Hurrah."

Abigail didn't respond. She was too busy thinking.

Maybe Rachel hadn't been lying after all.

Maybe this entire time the liar had been James.

He had motive. He even admitted that himself just yesterday. In no uncertain words, James said he wanted Rachel off the case. Would he have been capable of doing something to her? It had been pretty clear that night that Rachel had no intentions of leaving the case alone.

Abigail's chest grew taut as she recalled James's temper with the collector several days back. When it came to burying the pain caused by his mother's murderer, the use of physical force didn't seem to be beneath him.

Abigail whipped out her phone. She still didn't know much about the motel murder, but she knew who she should question about Rachel's disappearance.

As she composed a text to James, she tried to think of a public place to approach him, a place he'd willingly meet up with her without getting suspicious. If she was going to confront the guy on her own, she wanted to have a few witnesses nearby, just in case.

She looked up at Sally and Dag. "Sorry, but I gotta cut this short."

Sally lowered her sketchbook. "You've got a lead, don't you?"

"Not sure. But if something happens to me, you tell Grandma that I had left to go meet James at the park." With that, Abigail grabbed Thor's leash and the two hurried off.

CHAPTER EIGHTEEN

Abigail found her way to the local park. James had answered her text immediately, telling her he'd meet her at the swings. The park was a wide open space, with plenty of room for running around and shouting, which was exactly what a horde of children were doing. Abigail wasn't sure any of them were even playing a cohesive game. They just looked like they enjoyed chaos.

She found James sitting on a swing alone, eating an ice cream. Strawberry. Abigail was sure of it. She eyed the cone suspiciously as she closed in on her target.

"Hey there, Cupcake," James called when he spotted her. "Want to give me a push?"

"Not really." Abigail stopped in front of him, her back to the screaming kids. Thor sat at her side, and the two of them equally eyed James.

"All right," he began. "What did you want to talk to me about?"

"I honestly don't want to talk about it, but I have to know…"

He looked down at his cone. "Sure, strawberry's an unconventional choice, but then again, I'm rather unconventional myself."

"I'm not talking about your ice cream. I'm talking about Rachel."

James went very still.

Abigail continued, "What happened to your mother should never have happened to anyone. After all these years, you should be allowed to put the past behind you. But Rachel wouldn't let you do that."

James shook his head. "I suppose not."

"For the sake of her career, she dredged up an awful past, bringing up feelings both you and your dad wanted to put behind you. Evidence or not, she wanted her original story to be true. In the process, she kept rubbing salt into those old wounds, making things worse for your father."

"She did."

"Then there's last night. She approached you, you lost it, she lost it, and all those pent up feelings came out."

James steadied himself in the swing. "Do you think I have something to do with her going missing?"

"I don't know, James. I hope not."

He looked her in the eyes, his face unreadable. "Well, it's a good thing I have an alibi, then."

"You do?"

"I wasn't even in town when she disappeared. Right after I saw you and Granny, I left for Turtle Bay to do some deeper investigating. I had managed to talk a few of the motel guests into meeting with me at a bar last night to go over things. I even checked into the motel down there, Turtle Heights. I just got back this morning."

"You mean you talked to the guests from the wedding the victim was supposed to go to?"

"Yep. And I learned something interesting." James gestured toward the empty swing beside him. "Step into my office and I'll tell you all about it."

Abigail studied James's face. He seemed relaxed. Chipper even. Not exactly the face of a guy trying to get away with a crime. Without a word, she dropped into the swing next to him, with Thor sitting at her side.

James finished his ice cream cone and wiped his hands on his pants. "I acquired a list of wedding guests from my dad. When I was a kid on the streets of Wallace Point, I never thought I'd say this, but sometimes it's good to have a cop for a father." He pulled out a crumpled piece of paper from his trench coat pocket. "Look, here's the list of wedding guests. I know it's been a while, but sometimes that gives people a chance to remember something good, you know? A few of the guests had time to talk to me, so I followed up with them yesterday."

Abigail inwardly wondered how convenient it was that

he happened to check up on these old leads the night a woman he argued with had gone missing.

As if he could read her thoughts, James handed her the list. "Question them yourself, if you'd like. But if you want to save some time, I could just tell you what I found."

"And what's that?"

"A lot of what they said was stuff the police already knew. But this time I pursued a line of questions about the wedding rehearsal, which happened before the murder took place. They said that the bride and groom were both acting strange."

"Strange how?"

"Apparently the bride looked like she had been crying. And the groom looked angry. They hardly talked to each other the entire night."

"I guess that is weird," Abigail admitted. "What did the guests think about it?"

"They thought it was stress or nerves. They all felt like they had to tell me about their own weddings, or other weddings they'd been to. The point was, a lot of brides and grooms get pretty freaked out just before the big day. It's normal to see odd behavior."

"But this time, someone ended up dead."

James smirked at Abigail. "You said that just like a detective from one of those classic films I used to watch."

"Used to?"

"Anyway, I'm glad you decided to corner me about the case. I've hit a wall, and I'm starting to think you can help. So take that list, and if you find anything interesting, you let me know. Deal?"

James held out his hand. Abigail hesitated for a second before reaching out and shaking it. "Deal."

"Great. Hopefully you can read my handwriting. I've been told it's quite atrocious."

Abigail looked over the list to see that his handwriting was, in fact, chicken scratch. But she managed to make out enough of the letters as she scanned the list of names with their corresponding phone numbers and addresses.

Abigail folded the list neatly and placed it into the pocket of her jeans. "You'll be hearing from me."

James laughed. "I'm sorry I wasn't the one who kidnapped that reporter, Cupcake. I'll buy you an ice cream cone if that'd make you feel better?"

Abigail stood up. "No, thanks. Grandma's expecting me any minute."

James shrugged. "Suit yourself." He leaned back in the swing and pushed off with his feet.

Abigail turned to head back home, Thor following at her side. So, she didn't get far in discovering what happened to Rachel, but at least she had a list of names now. Fresh clues could mean a fresh look at the motel murder. All she had to do was connect the dots.

CHAPTER NINETEEN

Abigail read the list while she walked home. It included about a dozen wedding guests, and at the bottom of the page James had scrawled the names of the bride, groom, and victim: Monica Ives, Frank Davis, and Theodore Howard. After she read through the names a couple of more times, she folded the list and put it back in her pocket.

She and Thor headed up the front porch and made their way inside.

"Abigail?" Grandma's voice drifted into the front room. "Is that you?"

"It's me, Grandma."

Grandma was in the back room next to a cluster of antique lamps, a duster in one hand. She had tucked her white hair under a scarf so that only a few fluffy curls peeked out at the front. Missy sat by her feet, watching her human with adoring, attentive eyes. She looked away just long enough to wag her tail at Abigail.

"Grandma, you look like a housewife straight from the 1950s."

"Why, thank you. Some of my fondest memories are from the 50s. Now, what have you been up to all day?"

"Well, Thor and I met with Sally this morning. We walked to the Lafayette, and we caught up with Dag while Sally did some sketching."

"Sally's an artist?"

"Not if you ask her. Though I think she's pretty good, from the few sketches she let me see."

"Ah." Grandma's bright eyes sparkled. "I'll just have to pop over there one of these days and demand to see a few of those sketches."

"You'll embarrass her, Grandma."

"Of course I will. Embarrassing the youngsters is one of the great pleasures of old age. You'll love it, trust me."

Abigail shook her head, choosing to skip the part of her day where she had confronted James. "So that's what I was up to. How did your day go?"

"It was lovely! The Granny Gang and I made a few sock monkeys. But mostly we just sat around drinking tea and knitting. You were gone a while though. Were you out with Sally this whole time?"

Abigail had hoped Grandma wouldn't ask. After all, she had cornered one of Grandma's favorite people and accused him of foul play. "Well, I met James at the park."

Grandma's eyes grew wide. "You did?"

"Now, Grandma, we only met to talk about the case."

Grandma threw up her hands. "I didn't say anything, dear. Did you learn anything new?"

"A little. James interviewed some of the guests again, and they all said that the bride and groom were acting pretty strange at the rehearsal. They wouldn't talk to each other, and the bride looked like she'd been crying."

Grandma considered this information. "It could be nothing. A lot of couples get pre-wedding day jitters."

"Yeah, but for this couple, one of their guests ended up dead."

"What an awful way to kick off a marriage."

"It would have been," Abigail agreed, "if they hadn't canceled the wedding."

Grandma sighed. "I'm about finished dusting. Interested in an early supper?"

"That would be great, my stomach's been growling for the past ten minutes."

"Let's wash up, then. We can make dinner together and watch another old movie while we eat, even if it isn't Friday."

"I very much like that idea."

While Grandma got dinner started, Abigail headed up to the attic to retrieve the box of old movies. Soon, Grandma and Abigail were on the couch with a thick blanket over their knees and bowls of chili on their laps. Between them on the sofa was a plate of fresh, buttered cornbread. Missy and Thor sat on the floor, sniffing the air hopefully.

"Hey, Grandma." Abigail grabbed the remote and clicked on the old television. "Do the names Theodore Howard or Monica Ives sound familiar at all?"

"Theodore Howard or Monica Ives. Theodore sounds familiar. Why do you ask?"

"Theodore was the motel victim, so maybe you picked up his name in the newspapers. Monica Ives was the bride."

"Who was the groom?"

"Frank Davis."

"Hmm," Grandma mused. "Monica sounds vaguely familiar, but I don't know why. Frank Davis doesn't ring a bell."

Abigail shook her head. "The names are familiar to me too. I don't know if it's just because they might have been in the paper, or if I've seen them somewhere else."

"Don't think too hard about it, dear. Your brain will figure it out for you if you let it."

"You're probably right."

Abigail pressed the play button on the remote, wondering if Grandma would be able to make it through the movie this time.

To Abigail's surprise, Grandma did pretty well. Despite the food, the nearby crackling fire, and the warm doggy bodies that eventually snuggled between them, Grandma made it three-quarters of the way through the film before nodding off.

Abigail turned off the television and helped her sleepy grandmother up the stairs and to her bed. When she came back down, she washed their dinner dishes and tidied up the living room. The box of old VHS tapes needed to go back in the attic, but Abigail decided she could take care of that in the morning.

She was just about to turn off the light and head upstairs when her brain clicked. "Monica!"

Abigail rushed back into the living room and to the box of tapes. A few of the tapes were old films, but most of them were home movies that Abigail's mom had made as a teenager. And on these movies were labels, with various names on them, most likely childhood friends.

Abigail rummaged through the box, reading the descriptions hand written on the front of each tape until she found the one labeled 'Monica and Teddy.'

Feeding the tape into the VCR, Abigail sat back and watched the screen. At first there was only gray static, but after a few seconds a scene flickered up on the screen.

Sarah Lane's much younger face filled the screen. "Okay," she giggled. "We're going to catch the two lovebirds in the act." Another girlish giggle cracked through the speakers, but it wasn't from Sarah. It was someone else who hadn't yet come into view.

Abigail wasn't surprised. Her mother would have wanted all the attention on her.

The camera shifted clumsily, capturing dirt, shoes, and tree trunks before landing on two fuzzy figures on a swing set. After a moment, the camera focused.

Two teens, a girl and a boy, sat on a pair of swings. The

girl had bright red hair. The boy was tall and gangly. They rocked gently two and fro, linked by their hands.

"Is he gonna do it?" a voice asked. Abigail guessed it was her mother's accomplice. It sounded vaguely familiar.

"Shh! Of course he's going to do it. Look! There he goes."

The camera wobbled and then focused again. The tall boy was leaning toward the red-head, who sat very still.

"Jeez," Sarah giggled. "Monica looks like a statue. And Teddy looks like a bean pole."

Teddy, who had been frozen in place, suddenly gathered his wits, pecked Monica on the lips, and immediately straightened back up in his swing.

Sarah and her unseen accomplice broke into peals of laughter. Teddy and Monica must have heard them, because they looked in the direction of the camera. Sarah and her friend yelped, and the camera began to jostle wildly. The image transformed into a jumble of color: brown dirt, green shrubs, and scuffed blue sneakers.

For a split second, the image on the screen rushed toward the ground. Then everything went black.

Abigail grabbed her phone and called James.

"Hello?" James said. His voice was scratchy and his words were slurred.

"Monica Ives dated Theodore Howard."

"Cupcake? Why are you calling so late?"

"I just told you. Monica Ives dated Theodore Howard when they were teens." Abigail glanced at the clock on the mantelpiece. "And it's only nine. Nine is early."

"Yeah, well, some of us need our beauty sleep. So, you're saying that—"

"The bride-to-be dated the murder victim. Or, they were in some sort of relationship when they were younger, anyway."

"How do you know?"

"My mom took a video of their first kiss. I just watched it."

"Okay. So Monica dated Theodore. Monica was going to marry Frank. Theodore goes to the wedding rehearsal. Someone kills Theodore."

"I don't know exactly what it means yet, but it feels crucial somehow. What do you think?"

"I think that jealousy is a very common motive."

"You mean Frank? But why would he be jealous of such an old relationship? Unless..."

"Unless there was some sort of funny business still going on," James finished with a sigh. "Okay, let me run a scenario by you. Theodore and Monica had a thing as kids. They grow up, go their separate ways. Monica meets Frank, one thing leads to another, and then they're engaged. Now Theodore gets invited to the wedding. Old feelings flare up. Maybe he and Monica kiss. Maybe it's worse. Whatever happens, Frank finds out. He finds out just before his wedding."

"That would explain why the couple was acting so strange. According to the people you interviewed, he was upset and she was crying, right?"

"Right. So Frank gets mad, real mad. The next day, Theodore is dead and the wedding is called off." He was silent for a moment before announcing, "I think you may have uncovered a motive and a suspect."

Abigail took a deep breath, exhausted all of a sudden.

"Catching criminals is hard brain work, isn't it?" James chuckled, though there wasn't much joy in it. "Still think nine is early?"

"Not too early, at least."

"I'm going to revisit all the information we gathered so I can present a case to my father. Won't be until the morning though."

"Yeah, another night won't make a difference when the killer's been free for over a month now. Keep me in the loop, okay?"

"Of course. You do the same."

"Goodnight, James."

"Goodnight, Cupcake."

THE NEXT MORNING, while Grandma was helping a customer, James called Abigail.

She headed to the kitchen for some privacy. "Got some news?"

"I do."

"What's up?"

"I did some digging and found the make and model of

Frank's car, along with his license plate. I took it over to my dad first thing and he checked the CCTV footage from the motel. Frank's car was in the motel parking lot the night of the murder."

Abigail mulled over the details for a moment before saying, "Okay, but I'm curious about one thing."

"What's that?" James asked, his tone intrigued.

"Why was the murder so similar to a Ripper killing?"

"Ah. Well, let's not forget, it was Rachel who ran with that story. The cops never suspected the Ripper, much less mentioned him. She just got a few details about the stabbing and jumped to conclusions in hopes she was breaking a big story."

"Oh. I guess that makes sense." Abigail leaned against the kitchen counter. "Okay, so what happens now?"

"Now the police take the groom in for questioning. Let's hope that's the end of it."

"Let's. Thanks for the update. I'm gonna tell Grandma the good news."

"I'm sure she'll be relieved. I know my dad is. Anyhow, talk later." He hung up.

Abigail let out a long, relieved breath. They still didn't have every detail, but the case had to be close to solved now that they knew the groom had a motive and was at the scene of the crime. He very well could have had something to do with Rachel's disappearance too. Now they just needed a confession so Wallace Point could finally go back to being its quiet, quaint, wonderful self.

CHAPTER TWENTY

Abigail filled Grandma in on the details, starting from her a-ha moment last night, to her call with James, and ending with the critical clue found in the CCTV footage. Grandma could only shake her head. "Goodness. How could we miss something so obvious?"

"I think Rachel and her Ripper reports set the whole investigation back. Not that she deserves to be missing, but she really muddied up everything for the sake of a good story."

"At least it's just about solved now," Grandma said, but she hardly sounded relieved.

Abigail was about to take inventory of a box of old comics when Grandma came up from behind and tapped her shoulder. She looked up. "Yes, Grandma?"

"Abigail, dear, why don't we invite James and Willy over to dinner this evening?"

Abigail set the vintage comics down, wondering how any work got done with all the social engagements Grandma liked to rustle up. "Okay, I guess. Got something on your mind?"

"Not really. But the police will have interrogated the groom by then, right? Maybe they'll have some good news. Besides, I like knowing the details before everyone else."

"Good point. A nice big dinner might get them talking."

When they closed for lunch, Grandma called Sheriff Wilson and extended the invitation. He accepted, and Grandma immediately started planning a menu. She had plenty of time, since business was still sluggish. An hour before closing time, Grandma put Abigail in charge of the store while she started dinner.

Abigail had no objections. A couple of times throughout the day, she'd caught herself wishing for tourist season to begin. She didn't admit this to Grandma, of course. But tourists meant more customers, and more customers meant more sales.

It wasn't that she didn't like the quiet days with Grandma. She loved them, actually. But she worried about Grandma's finances, and Sally's, and all the other small businesses in Wallace Point. Running a store in a tourist town was tough work during the off seasons.

James and Sheriff Wilson arrived just as Abigail was about to lock up for the day. Sheriff Wilson was still in his uniform. James wore his customary rumpled shirt, pants, and trench coat. They both had a satisfied look on their faces.

"Hey, Sheriff Wilson, James," Abigail greeted. "You two look happy."

James smirked. "Well, we should be, Cupcake. I think we've just about wrapped this case up. What is that incredible smell?"

"Grandma's been cooking up a storm. I think you're in for a treat."

Abigail let the two men in and locked up behind them while Thor thoroughly sniffed their shoes and hands. When he didn't find anything objectionable, the Great Dane stepped back, as if granting his permission. Missy zipped out of the kitchen, allowed them to lean down and scratch her behind the ears, then zipped right back.

"Granny Lane," James called, tailing the little Shih Tzu. "When you said dinner, I thought you meant ordering out pizza. You didn't have to do all this."

"Oh, James, it was nothing," Grandma said, stepping away from the stove for a hug. "I've had a hankering to make a big southern meal. You two just provided me with a good excuse."

James let go of Grandma and looked around the kitchen. "Can I help at all?"

"Not a bit. You three sit down at the table. We're anxious to hear everything about today's interrogation."

"Now, Florence," Sheriff Wilson began as he dropped into

a chair. "You know we're not supposed to talk about what happens at the station."

"Don't you dare try that on me, William Wilson. How many times have you come to me for advice in the past?"

"And you wouldn't have even picked up the groom if it wasn't for my tip," Abigail pointed out while taking her seat across from James.

James shook his head. "You may as well give them what they want, Dad. The Lane women always get what they want."

"Well, all right," Sheriff Wilson relented. "But nothing we say leaves this room."

Grandma frowned. "Willy, I don't know what's gotten into you. While I'm a gossip about the small details, you know I always keep the big things to myself."

"Come now, Florence. I'm just trying to uphold the law."

Grandma huffed. "As if I'm not an upstanding citizen?"

"Why don't I just go ahead and start from the top," James jumped in, sharing an impatient look with Abigail. "We brought the groom in early this morning, just after I called you, Abigail. Suffice it to say, he was pretty bewildered as we walked him into the interrogation room."

"Wait," Abigail said. "You were allowed to be part of the interrogation? But you're not even a police officer."

"I was today. My dad made me a temporary deputy. It's one of the perks of being a sheriff."

"Okay. Then what happened?"

"So we asked Frank about the murder of one of his

wedding guests, and he had the nerve to act like he never heard of Teddy. Not sure how you *don't* know the name of your own murdered wedding guest."

Abigail frowned. "That's pretty odd."

James continued. "And the guy's excuse was that he had been dealing with personal drama. 'My wedding fell apart,' and blah, blah, blah. As if he could somehow miss the fact that a murder happened."

"Did he say anything about Rachel Cuthbert?"

"He said the same thing he said about the victim. He didn't know who she was, never heard her name before."

"All right, James," Grandma interrupted. "I could use your help now. These platters are heavier than I remembered."

James jumped up, and so did Abigail. Between the two of them, they carried everything to the table. Abigail then grabbed a pitcher of iced tea and poured everyone a glass before returning to her seat.

"Florence." Sheriff Wilson's face lit up like a kid's on Christmas morning. "You've outdone yourself."

Grandma had whipped together a good old southern dinner. She had baked the macaroni and cheese so that the bread crumbs on top were golden brown and slightly crunchy, while the cheese underneath was piping hot and creamy. She had also made mashed potatoes, garlicky green beans, skillet cornbread, and pan-fried chicken.

They all heaped their plates high with comfort food, and for the next few minutes no one spoke. They were all too focused on their dishes to think about anything else.

SHELLY WEST

Abigail finally broke the silence. "Do you believe him? About Rachel Cuthbert."

"He hasn't budged on that one," Sheriff Wilson said with a shrug.

James added, "But as far as the original murder goes, we caught a break. See, just the CCTV footage wasn't enough. That got him in for questioning, but now we can keep him in custody."

"What was the break?" Grandma asked.

"Another wedding guest called the police station," Sheriff Wilson explained. "They passed the call along to me. This was one of the guests James had followed up with. She said she had thought of something that might be important."

"She told Dad that the groom knew the victim. Not only that, but that Frank really didn't like Theodore. That they had a couple of scuffles back in high school, even."

"You're kidding," Abigail said. "What perfect timing."

James nodded. "You're telling us. So we went back in there and confronted him, but Frank still claimed he never knew Theodore for a good thirty minutes before he finally caved."

Abigail set down her fork. "So he admitted it?"

"Well, he admitted to thinking Theodore was a scumbag, and that he was ashamed to have ever associated with him. But then he claimed he'd never kill Theodore. Maybe deck him, but not kill him."

"Then where does that leave the investigation?" Grandma asked.

"It's not looking good for him, I'll tell you that much. Again, Frank has motive and opportunity. His car was at the motel, and we caught him lying about knowing the victim." James shook his head. "At best, the guy has a case of classic disassociation. He probably can't accept the fact that he murdered someone. Probably did the reporter in too for asking too many questions. Not sure we'll ever get our hands on the murder weapon, but the rest of the evidence is pretty solid."

Abigail nibbled on a piece of cornbread. The case against Frank Davis seemed pretty solid, even though the murder weapon still hadn't been found. She was relieved, but she also wondered why James was so ready to accept an idea like disassociation. Maybe, like her, he wanted to have the case resolved.

It really didn't seem like James or his father were really pursuing what happened to Rachel. Sure, she was a pain in their sides, but wasn't time of the essence in missing person cases?

Abigail sighed. She had to be patient. They knew what they were doing, and Frank most likely had the answers. It was simply a matter of waiting him out.

CHAPTER TWENTY-ONE

The morning was overcast and windy. Instead of a walk, Abigail chose to sit on the porch with Thor by her side, watching the clouds roll by as the sky darkened with every minute. The neighborhood was particularly quiet that morning. Camille wasn't in her garden, and the handful of other walkers or runners that Abigail usually crossed paths with were nowhere to be seen.

For once, Wallace Point looked deserted, like a town quietly abandoned in the wake of an apocalypse. She half expected a zombie to amble down the street at any moment.

After a while, Abigail and Thor headed back inside to find Grandma banging about in the kitchen. Missy yipped a little greeting as they walked into the room.

"Hey, Grandma. What are you up to?"

"Good morning, dear. I'm just putting up the dishes you

washed last night. After that feast, I'm feeling like something rather light for breakfast. What do you think?"

"Light sounds great, Grandma. I didn't run today, so I'm not too hungry anyhow."

"Eggs and English muffins sound all right?"

"Sounds perfect. I'm going to change clothes then I'll be right back down."

"No rush, dear. I suspect it will be another quiet morning here at the store. The police need to announce they've caught the killer already, for the sake of this town's economy."

"Yeah, no kidding. Be back in a second."

Abigail headed up to get dressed and brush her hair out of her face. When she picked up her phone just before heading back downstairs, she noticed she had a voicemail from James.

"That's weird," she said aloud, dropping onto her bed beside Thor while she played back the message. Why would James call her so early? Had Frank confessed?

"Hey, Abigail," James's voice drifted into her ear. Her stomach tightened. James hardly ever called her by her name, and his voice sounded heavy and dull.

"Sorry to call so early," the message continued. "I just, uh… Well, there's been a development in the case that has caught everyone by surprise. I think I'd like to run it by you, see what you think. Just… call me back as soon as you can. This is James, by the way."

Abigail shook her head. Whatever James wanted to tell

her didn't sound like it would be particularly pleasant. But what could he have to say? The case was just about wrapped up.

A knock sounded at her door. "Abigail? Are you about ready, dear? I can keep breakfast warm in the oven if you'd like a few more minutes."

"Come in, Grandma," Abigail called.

Grandma opened the door. Missy darted into the room and hopped up onto the bed, squeezing her body between Abigail and Thor. "Everything all right, Abigail?"

"I'm not sure, but I'm about to find out. James left me a weird voicemail. I'm going to call him back."

"I can leave you alone if you'd like."

"Don't. I think this is about the case. Here, let me play the message on speaker so you can hear it."

Grandma listened to the voicemail. Her eyebrows furrowed in confusion. "My, my, he's mysterious this morning, isn't he?"

Abigail shrugged, then dialed James's number, keeping the phone on speaker.

"Hello?" James croaked, his voice sounding tired.

"Hey, James. It's Abigail. And Grandma's here too."

James sighed. "Hey, you two."

"Is this a bad time?"

"Maybe, but I don't think there'll be a good time at any point today."

"Okay, that's mysterious. And alarming. What's going on?"

"We found Rachel Cuthbert."

Abigail's heart thumped in her chest as she and Grandma shared wide eyed looks. "Oh, wow. Is she... Is she okay?"

"Let me rephrase that," James said. "She actually found us. She was waiting at the station this morning when Dad arrived."

Abigail was losing patience over James's trickle of information. Even Grandma was starting to tap her small foot. "Okay, James. Hurry up and tell us what's going on."

On the other line, James sighed again. "She confessed to the motel murder."

Abigail dropped the phone on her bed. She scrambled to pick it back up while Grandma wrung a kitchen towel she had been holding.

"Hello?" James was saying. "Abigail, are you there?"

"I'm here, James. I, uh, wasn't expecting that."

"Neither was I, or anyone else for that matter."

"So, what did she say?"

"Well, she's not saying much. All she keeps saying is that she did it, that she was the copycat killer. She showed up here covered in dirt and leaves. She looked as if she had been lost in the woods for a week."

"Does she seem all right?"

"Yeah. She doesn't seem to be injured in any way. But here's the kicker." James paused. "She turned in the murder weapon."

"What?" Abigail gasped.

Grandma's mouth popped open. "Oh my heavens."

"Yeah, she just handed it to Dad in a paper bag. It's… It's not just any knife." James paused, then cleared his throat. "It's the original knife the Wallace Point Ripper used."

"James, I'm so sorry. She handed it to your dad?" Abigail saw Grandma tear up and then turn away. "How did she get her hands on it? The collector said he sold it."

"He sold it to her. Rachel Cuthbert bought that knife off him a week before the murder. It turns out that she fits into our 'technologically savvy' suspect profile. She runs the newspaper's website, and it seems her talents extend to using untraceable digital currency."

Abigail froze. Just last night she had been concerned for Rachel Cuthbert's well-being. Now, the reporter had reappeared and confessed to having committed the murder she had written about. Even worse, she turned in the weapon that had taken the lives of several Wallace Point residents, including James's mom.

Grandma asked, "How are you and your dad holding up?"

"Dad's not doing well. I mean, he's glad to have her in custody, sure. But seeing the knife, holding it in his own hands… Yeah, he's not doing well. I guess I'm not either."

Abigail offered, "James, if you or your dad need to talk, come see us. We'll be here all day, with plenty of good food and warm drinks."

Grandma nodded her approval.

"Thanks, Abigail. I don't know if Dad will feel much like seeing anyone. He's already gone home for the day, actually. I think I might come over, though."

"We'll be here, whenever you're ready."

"Thanks. Anyway, I gotta... Well... I should go. Bye, ladies." He abruptly hung up.

Abigail shook her head and looked up at Grandma. "Of all the officers Rachel could have handed over the knife to..."

"Poor Willy," Grandma murmured. "I can't imagine how he feels right now." She stepped closer to Abigail. "I'm going to work on a casserole to send back with James. Otherwise, I will worry that Willy won't eat anything today." Grandma reached out and smoothed Abigail's hair. "I'm glad you're here, sweetie."

Abigail looked up into her grandmother's eyes, found her hand, and gave it a gentle squeeze. "I'm glad I'm here too."

Grandma smiled then picked Missy up before heading back downstairs, but Abigail lingered in her room, petting Thor while she mulled over the news. So, Frank hadn't killed Theodore. At least, that was what Rachel wanted them to believe. But why would she kill Theodore herself? What motive could she possibly have had?

CHAPTER TWENTY-TWO

The morning dragged by. Usually on slow days Grandma and Abigail found plenty to keep themselves busy. They often rearranged their wares into different displays, or dusted and polished until every piece gleamed. Recently, Abigail had even started cataloging Grandma's knowledge about her antiques; she racked Grandma's brain for every tidbit of information, then copied it all down onto index cards which she attached to the respective item. When all else failed, they pulled out the newspaper and worked on a crossword together.

This morning, however, neither one of them had the heart for any of their usual activities. Abigail slumped over the counter, staring at nothing, while Thor watched her with a sad look in his big, dark eyes. Grandma sat in an armchair on display, absently tugging on Missy's ears while the dog slept on her lap.

Neither of them felt very hungry around lunch time, and they had just about decided to skip the meal and carry on brooding, when Thor decided he'd had enough.

The Great Dane got to his feet and trotted over to Abigail. He sat and stared up at her for a minute. When that failed to get her attention, he tucked his head into her lap and gave her his best puppy dog eyes. That trick only earned him a brief pat on the head.

Determined to help his human no matter what, Thor loped back around to the front of the counter and began to moan like a dying old man.

"You okay, Thor?" Abigail asked, but her eyes weren't focused on him. They were focused on something far away that he couldn't see. So, he groaned more dramatically, and he continued to do so until he finally got her to look at him. "Thor? What's wrong?"

Thor sauntered to the front door and pulled his leash from a nearby basket.

"I don't feel much like going for a walk."

Thor barked.

"I said no."

Thor barked again, louder.

Grandma looked up then, as if she had just arrived from somewhere a million miles away. "What's wrong with him?"

"Thor really wants to go for a walk, it seems."

Missy jumped down from Grandma's lap and scurried over to join Thor.

Grandma frowned. "Missy? What are you doing? You hate going on walks."

Missy sneezed and also pulled her leash out of the basket.

Abigail looked at Grandma. "I think our dogs are ganging up on us."

Grandma sighed, a soft smile pulling at the corners of her mouth. "We better listen to them, then."

"I guess we should. A walk might be helpful anyway. I don't think we'd be very good company for James if he showed up just now."

"I'll write up a sign for the door."

In no time, Grandma, Abigail, and their dogs were outside, strolling up and down the quiet sidewalks. Thor, out of consideration for the huffing, puffing Missy, set an easy pace.

There wasn't much to see in the neighborhood. It was lunchtime on a weekday, and most of their neighbors were not at home. But overhead, the sun shone bright in a blue sky dotted with white, puffy clouds. The breeze was cold and invigorating, and the exercise helped shake them out of their slump. By the time they circled back to the store, Grandma and Abigail were feeling refreshed and better equipped to face a tough day.

They arrived not a moment too soon; James walked in five minutes later. His curly brown hair was even wilder than usual, and he had dark circles under his eyes.

Without a word, Grandma walked over to James and put her arms around the broad-shouldered man she'd known since he was a baby. James, his face grim, hugged her back, gently yet firmly.

"I'll whip up some of my special cookies," Grandma said as she pulled away. "You two stay here. Can't have you stealing my secret recipe."

Abigail smiled, thinking of the container of store-bought cookie dough sitting in the refrigerator.

"Sure thing, Granny Lane." James lowered himself into the armchair Grandma and Missy had been using. Thor, sensing another human in need, parked himself at James's feet. James looked up at Abigail as he pet the dog. "Slow day?"

Abigail nodded. "It's been slow since the murder at the motel. Tourist season is just around the corner, though."

"Tourists," James said, shaking his head. "I remember hating them as a kid. But I did eventually come to like them. Meeting all sorts of different people from all sorts of places is fun."

"I can see that," Abigail said. She wondered when or if James would bring up Rachel Cuthbert, but she certainly wasn't going to broach the subject unless he was ready. "I'm sure I'll get to meet some fascinating characters when the Christmas season rolls around."

James snorted. "I remember when a full-time mime came to town once."

"You mean he made a living miming?"

"It was a she, actually. Whether she made a living, I can't say. But I can say she never broke character."

Abigail frowned. "Not once?"

"We never heard her speak, and we never saw her without her face paint. She did manage to save another tourist from falling off a pier into the water, though. She even jumped a few invisible hurdles before catching him. Quite the sight."

Grandma bustled into the room carrying a tray laden with cookies and coffee. "Here we are." She placed the tray on the checkout counter, and James pushed himself out of his seat to partake.

The rich aroma of the strong coffee mingled with the sweet scent of the cookies. James smiled. "Thanks, Granny Lane. I think this is exactly what I needed after this morning."

"I'm sorry again for what happened. How's Willy?"

"He's struggling now, but he held it together while he was at the station. He took the knife into evidence and started processing Cuthbert. He only went home after he tied up all the loose ends."

"You two may not see this so much, now that Willy is old and gray like me, but Willy Wilson is made of tough stuff. He's where you get your grit from, James."

James looked away. "He shouldn't have to be made of tough stuff anymore. He should get to live his life in peace, doing what he loves for the town he loves. But thanks to a fame-seeking reporter, peace is the last thing he'll have for a while."

"So you think she did it purely for the publicity?" Abigail asked.

"Why else would she kill a guy with the same murder weapon as the Wallace Point Ripper? Why else would she cover the story as if the Ripper had re-emerged after years in hiding? When I think of the things that woman has done, the people she has hurt, all for the sake of her stupid career..." James shook his head.

"It just doesn't make sense to me," Abigail admitted. "I mean, Rachel isn't the most scrupulous person. She was friends with my mom, if that tells you anything. But to kill a man just for her career? And the timing of the murder, the wedding, and then the wedding being called off—the love triangle thing can't be coincidence."

James sighed. "Frank is no longer a suspect, not when someone else walks in and confesses. I just don't understand why Rachel had to bring back the Ripper. That was a terrible time in Wallace Point. Why not make up a new killer?"

"She was probably one of his fans," Grandma said with a shrug.

Abigail and James glanced at each other, and then at Grandma. Abigail asked, "What do you mean one of his fans, Grandma?"

"Oh, I remember the oddest craze going through this town after the Wallace Point Ripper case had officially gone cold."

"What do you mean?" James asked.

"Well, many of the local teenagers started fantasizing about him. Especially the girls. I think you were too young to have known about it."

Abigail grimaced. "Fantasizing about the Ripper?"

"Yes. Even your mother. She told me that he was misunderstood, that his victims deserved it. Can you believe that?"

Abigail and James shared another look. She had no idea what he was thinking, but she'd just been struck by a thought. "James, I think I need some air. Join me out on the porch?"

Abigail was certain James didn't know what she was up to, but he didn't miss a beat. "Air sounds great. We'll be right back, Granny Lane."

Grandma nodded. "Take your mugs with you. It's cold out there."

Out on the porch, James cradled his hot coffee in his gloved hands. "Something's on your mind, Cupcake."

"Yeah, but I'm not sure exactly what."

"Tell me."

"All I know is that something doesn't feel right about Rachel's confession. I'm not saying she didn't do it, but I don't think the story is complete. And then Grandma said that thing about the Wallace Point Ripper having a fan club. I'm just getting a feeling."

"You have a hunch," James explained. "All good PIs and detectives have them and pay attention to them. I'm convinced Rachel did this, but you've proven pretty handy so far, Cupcake. What do you want to do?"

"I want to call my mom, see what she can tell us about this fan club. You don't have to be here if you don't feel like listening to something like that. I just don't want to call her in front of Grandma. They don't have the greatest history."

James set his jaw. "I don't really want to hear about a fan club for my mother's murderer, but if you think it's important, then I will."

"She might not even pick up," Abigail warned. "She usually doesn't." Then she pulled out her phone and called her mom.

CHAPTER TWENTY-THREE

Abigail held her breath as the line connected. She wondered briefly if it had been a bad idea to call her mother. Not that Mom was likely to pick up, but if she did, who knew what dismissive thing she might say about the Ripper. The last thing Abigail wanted was to rub salt in James's wounds.

The phone rang three times until finally Sarah Lane picked up.

"Yes, dear?"

Abigail put the call on speaker phone so that James could hear right along with her. "Hey, Mom. Do you have a minute?"

"Five, to be exact. I'm on my smoke break."

"Okay, so Grandma says you used to have a crush on the Wallace Point Ripper. Is that true?"

Her mom broke into a fit of coughing and laughter. "Abi, you can't possibly think I have something to do with that murder."

"No, I don't. But I think you might know who does."

"How would I know? I haven't been anywhere near Wallace Point in years, thank goodness. And I certainly haven't kept up with any of the poor saps there."

Abigail tapped her foot. "Grandma said there was a bit of a fan club among the local teens back then. A group of kids who were really sympathetic toward the Ripper? And you were part of this group?"

"Yeah, that's right."

"Well, could you give me some names?"

James and Abigail listened intently as Sarah Lane took a long drag on her cigarette. "Well, there's that girl who ended up working at the newspaper. What's-her-face, with the dark hair."

James's eyebrows shot up. Abigail hurried to supply a name. "You mean Rachel. Rachel Cuthbert. Yeah, she even had the original knife. But who else?"

"Well, if anyone did it, it's her. Rachel was a weirdo. Absolutely crazy for the Ripper."

"Okay, Rachel Cuthbert loved the Ripper. Who else?"

"Calm down, hun. It's not easy thinking back that far. You're still too young to understand. Let's see. Was there a Francis? No, no, I don't think there was." Sarah took another drag. "Honestly, for me it was just a fad. I'll admit I got caught up in the romance of it all. The thought that he was misunderstood. So was I, you know. Misunderstood."

Abigail could see the muscles working in James's jaw. If she didn't get some answers from her mother soon, this phone call would end up being a painful waste of time for James.

"Okay, Mom. But who else worshipped the guy?"

"Oh, I've got it! It wasn't Francis. It was Frank! That's right, Frank. He was *such* a geek back then, and he just loved the Ripper."

"Was Frank's last name Davis?"

"That's right, it was. I'd just about forgotten. Anyhow, break's over. I'll talk to you later." Sarah abruptly disconnected the call.

Abigail gave James a look of triumph.

"How about that?" he mumbled. "Frank and Rachel, our two most suspicious suspects, knew each other way back in high school, and both were fans of the Ripper. So, could Rachel and Frank be in cahoots?"

"It makes sense. Frank finds out about Theodore's adolescent fling with his fiancée, thinks it's still going on. He wants revenge, but he needs to cover his tracks."

"Heck, the guy might even feel like getting clever." James paced up and down the front porch, his hands stuffed into the depths of his trench coat pockets, his shoulder hunched in concentration.

Abigail was surprised when she felt a sense of relief.

James was getting back to his old pesky, determined self—just the way Abigail could tolerate him.

"Frank finds out about Theodore," James said, picking up where Abigail had left off. "He wants revenge, but he needs to cover his tracks. Lucky for him, his old pal Rachel is still around. So, he sees a way he can get rid of Teddy without anyone tracing the murder back to him. And the icing on the cake is that he can pay homage to his old hero in the process."

"That would explain why the details of this murder didn't exactly match the Wallace Point Ripper's MO."

"Modus operandi." James grinned. "Good words for an amateur PI. You know, I could give you a few pointers."

Abigail rolled her eyes. "I hope you're not thinking I want to be your apprentice."

"I'll teach you everything I know, Cupcake. Stick with me, and you'll be the toast of the town."

"As I was saying, the murders don't exactly match because they weren't meant to. The motel murder was a rush job. He didn't have the time to remember all the original details."

"Or to execute them, for that matter. No pun intended, of course."

"It sounds like Rachel was the architect of Theodore's murder. She certainly didn't have the motive to kill Teddy specifically, but she had a career to grow."

James stared at his shoes. Abigail followed his gaze. Unlike the rest of his frumpy outfit, his shoes were actually quite nice and well-cared for.

"You know what the issue is, don't you?"

Abigail sighed. "The issue is solid proof."

Just then, James's phone buzzed. He dug it out of a pocket and glanced at the screen. "It's my dad." He shot a quick look at Abigail. "Do you mind?"

"Go for it."

James answered his phone and stepped off the porch.

Abigail watched him meander around the parking lot. She was glad her mom had miraculously picked up the phone, although she still didn't like knowing she'd been part of a serial killer fan club.

Granted, most teenagers went through some weird phases. For a while, Abigail had been obsessed with dog shows—the high end kind where breeders displayed canines with royal bloodlines. Abigail had refused to watch anything else on television for the longest time.

It drove her mom crazy, but Abigail learned a lot. In fact, that teenage obsession had come in handy a few years ago when she had been looking for a dog. She knew what a healthy dog looked like, and Thor fit the bill.

But a teenage obsession with a serial killer? Abigail couldn't see that leading to anything good. The present murder case seemed to be obvious proof of that.

James hung up and returned to the porch. "Bad news, Cupcake. The police are taking Rachel Cuthbert's confession at face value."

"What does that mean for the investigation?"

"Well, I can tell you they're officially releasing Frank Davis."

Abigail groaned. "I still think he's involved."

"I do too. But you know the issue."

"Solid proof."

James nodded. "I gotta head back to my motel room."

"You'll have to say goodbye to Grandma first, or else she'll worry. She also has a casserole she wants you to give to your father."

"Of course."

They stepped back inside, and Grandma regaled them with another fresh pot of coffee. James accepted another mug, then apologized. "Sorry, Granny Lane, but I gotta run. Either of you get any a-ha moments, you know who to call."

Abigail answered for the both of them, "We'll call. But you have to do the same."

"Deal."

"One moment!" Grandma said, hurrying off to grab the casserole she had made for Willy. James accepted the heavy dish before heading out.

Once James drove off, Grandma smiled. "He seems to be in a better mood."

"Yeah. We came up with a new direction for the case. I think having something to work on keeps him from dwelling."

"He's just like his dad, then. Willy loves to drown his worries with work."

"I think the cookies and coffee helped too."

"If there's one thing I've learned in all my years on this earth, it's that there's nothing fresh cookies and a good friend can't help heal."

Abigail smiled. She noticed Grandma said fresh cookies, not from-scratch cookies. Then she turned her thoughts to the case.

So it looked like Frank Davis was going to let Rachel take the fall for the murder. That didn't surprise Abigail much; she didn't expect a murderer to have scruples. But why would Rachel go along with it? What could she gain from confessing to a murder she wasn't fully responsible for?

CHAPTER TWENTY-FOUR

Early the next morning, Thor waited while Abigail sleepily tied her shoe laces. He had his leash in his mouth and a look of pure joy in his big eyes.

The soft tapping of little paws made them both look up. Missy walked primly up to the front door, her nose stuck high up in the air. She then did the oddest thing: She stepped over to the wicker basket and picked up her leash.

Thor thumped his tail against the floor, but Abigail rubbed her eyes, wondering whether she was dreaming.

"Missy?" she asked, fighting back a yawn. "What are you doing?"

Missy dropped her leash at Abigail's feet.

"But you hate going on walks. And you hate going outside. *And* you hate being away from Grandma. Are you sure?"

Missy sneezed, as if offended by Abigail's skepticism.

"All right. Just remember this was your idea, not mine."

Abigail finished tying her laces. She picked up both leashes, opened the door, and peeked out into the gray morning. With a deep breath, Abigail embarked, the two dogs at her side. They made a funny trio: a Great Dane with boundless enthusiasm, a Shih Tzu with a permanent puppy scowl, and a young woman who gasped as much as she jogged.

The neighborhood was quiet, as usual, but Camille was in her garden. Missy, who had never seen a human do an army crawl through a pumpkin patch while murmuring sweet nothings to growing gourds, exploded into a fit of yips. Thor joined in just for fun.

"Good morning, Abigail!" Camille called over the din. Her nose was covered in gold pollen dust. "Is the jogging getting any easier?"

Abigail stopped and braced herself against Camille's white picket fence. "Not really. How's the garden?"

"Magnificent. Just take a look at this beauty." Camille swept aside a carpet of foliage to reveal a pumpkin that was almost the size of Thor.

"Jeez, Camille, I think your pumpkin may have swallowed a child."

Camille grinned proudly. "Oh, this old thing? It's a baby compared to some of the other pumpkins I've grown in the past. I bet this fella is close to five hundred pounds."

"Five hundred! That's insane."

"Not really. That's about a quarter of the size some of the biggest pumpkins can get."

"What are you going to do with it?"

"Well, first I'm going to truck it into the school. The kids love posing with my giant pumpkins. Then I'll gut it and carve it into the creepiest thing I can imagine. The kids love that too. All of the innards will go to a group of teachers. We make seasoned pumpkin seeds and send them home with our students."

"Wow, that's really nice of you."

"It is, isn't it? I see you've got a new companion today."

"Yeah." Abigail squinted down at Missy. The Shih Tzu had flopped onto her side on the sidewalk. She panted heavily, and her tongue lolled out of her mouth. "We just started, but she's in even worse shape than me. For some reason she insisted on walking today."

"Maybe you should take it easy, let her build up some strength. We've all got to start somewhere."

"You're preaching to the choir, Camille. I'm always ready to stop running. It's Thor I'm worried about. He'd run all day if I let him."

Camille shot an appraising look at the big dog. "I'll bet. But Thor seems to be a gentleman at heart. I'm sure he'll understand."

"Well, that was all the convincing I needed. Thor, Missy, let's go home."

At the word home, Thor's tail drooped. He slunk back toward Abigail, glancing resentfully at Missy. The Shih Tzu didn't move. She just continued to lie on the cool sidewalk, panting.

"Come on, Missy. Let's go home."

Missy merely twitched a paw.

"I think she might need a lift," Camille said. She had her chin propped up on her enormous pumpkin as if it were a pillow.

"You've got to be kidding me," groaned Abigail. Still, she went over to the pile of fluff and peeled the little dog off the sidewalk. Missy stared at the sky beyond Abigail's head, refusing to make eye contact. Abigail shook her head. "I'll see you later, Camille."

"Sure thing. Give Granny Lane my love."

Abigail walked back to the store, Missy in her arms and Thor slinking along at her heels. When she made it home, Grandma was waiting for them at the door. She still wore her robe, and her hair was a lovely tangle of soft white curls.

"Missy, there you are," Grandma said, reaching out her arms to take the dog. "I was worried, you silly thing. What happened?"

Abigail shrugged. "Sorry, Grandma, but Missy insisted on coming with me this morning. I was surprised too."

"Missy wanted to go with you?"

"Yeah, isn't that weird?"

Grandma stared at Abigail, and then at Missy. She broke out into a loud, long cackle. "Missy, you vain thing."

"What's so funny, Grandma?"

"I think Missy's worried about her figure."

"What?"

Grandma doubled over with laughter, and soon she had to lower herself into a chair to catch her breath. "Honest to goodness, Abigail. I noticed she'd gained some weight, so I've been coming up with a few new nicknames: dough-baby, chubbykins, fluffmuffin. I didn't think too much of it until just last night. Can you believe I actually caught her scrutinizing herself in my mirror?"

"Grandma, there's no way."

"But I saw her, I'm telling you. She turned one way, and then another. She even looked over her shoulder at her little rump. When she caught me watching, she got all huffy." Grandma wiped a tear from her eye. "That must have pushed her over the edge."

"You're telling me Missy is trying to lose some weight? That's why she insisted on going on a run with us?"

Grandma nodded, still laughing too hard to stand. Abigail studied the dog. Missy did have a rather sheepish look on her little face.

"Well, she certainly didn't get very far. I had to peel her off the sidewalk. Literally."

Grandma broke into a fresh round of laughter, and she didn't stop until Missy jumped out of her lap and scurried away indignantly.

"You've done it now, Grandma. Missy's mad."

"Oh, go on and let her pout." Grandma finally stood, her eyes still wet with tears. "How does oatmeal with berries and cream sound for breakfast?"

"That sounds great. I'm going to run up and shower." Abigail took the stairs two at a time. She ducked into the bathroom and breezed back out twenty minutes later, fresh and clean and ready to tackle another day at the Whodunit Antiques checkout counter.

She was just about to head downstairs when she got a call from James. What did he want so early in the morning? Did he have another break in the case already?

"Good morning, James," Abigail answered.

"Good morning, Cupcake."

"Any new thoughts since last night?"

"Nope. You?"

"Oh, me neither."

"Well, guess I'm going to go stalk the groom now. You coming with me?

"Stalk the groom? How? And why?"

"When Frank was in for questioning, I put a tracker under his car."

"You what? Is that even legal?"

"I try not to worry about those kinds of things. All I know is that he stopped by his home in Turtle Bay after being released last night. Since early this morning, however, the car's been taking odd roads all over the outskirts of town, as if he were looking for something."

Abigail wished the police hadn't let Frank go. The guy was clearly involved, and yet he was wandering around free as a bird. "I wonder what he's doing?"

"I don't know, but we're running out of time. Now that

things are coming to a head, he might do something desperate, and soon."

"So, what do we do?"

"We'll tail him. You'll take your car, and I'll take mine."

Abigail frowned. "You want me to tail him in my yellow VW Bug? Don't you think that'd be incredibly obvious?"

"Exactly. And if you can get Thor in the passenger seat, even better. You'll act as a distraction, put a little pressure on him, make him a little paranoid, until you break off from our target's tracks. Then he'll think he's home free, all the while I'm following him the rest of the way, from much farther behind."

Abigail thought it over. Honestly, it sounded like fun. She'd never tailed a car before, but she figured this was a great way to start. The target, as James put it, was supposed to notice her, so she couldn't really mess it up.

"All right," she agreed. "But I need to let Grandma know. I'm supposed to help her at the store today."

"Sure thing, Cupcake. You just let me know when you're headed out. We can meet up at Sally's place. I'm parked outside, enjoying some donuts."

"Okay, give me a few."

After Abigail hung up and descended the stairs, she found Grandma waiting for her with a hot bowl of oatmeal.

Abigail sat down at the kitchen table. She grabbed the pitcher of warmed milk that sat by the bowls and poured a generous amount into her bowl.

"Would you mind taking Missy running with you again

tomorrow?" Grandma asked. "I shouldn't have made fun of her weight. I should be supporting her efforts to exercise."

"She's welcome to come with us." Abigail spooned a large bite of the creamy oats and strawberries into her mouth. "Hey Grandma, how do you feel about me taking off today?"

"Sure, honey," Grandma answered absently. She kept her attention on Missy, who picked delicately at her dog food.

"Great. I'll be taking the car and meeting James as soon as I finish breakfast."

Grandma looked up with sudden interest. "You're up to something, Miss Abigail."

"Yeah, a bit of PI work."

"Nothing dangerous, I hope?"

"Nothing more dangerous than taking on a bunch of pirates. And this time I'll have Thor with me."

Grandma cocked her head, considering. "Okay," she finally said. "Just be careful."

CHAPTER TWENTY-FIVE

Abigail and Thor sat in her bright yellow car, waiting for their target. "Any second now," James said over the speakers. Abigail had connected her phone to the car's speakers so that she could keep both her hands on the wheel while she tailed Frank.

She parked the car at an empty gas station. That station was the only sign of life at the four-way stop. Abigail and Thor would be impossible to miss once they pulled out of the lot and onto the road.

"Okay, there he is," James said. At the same time, a sleek charcoal sedan with tinted windows rolled up to the four-way stop. "Do you see him?"

"Yeah." Abigail shifted her car into reverse, backed out of her spot, then pulled out of the parking lot. "Did you say this was the third time Frank's passed this gas station?"

"Yep. I can't figure out what he's doing. He's been on the road for hours now."

The sedan made a slow right at the stop sign. Another car got between Abigail and her target, but she decided that was a good thing. Tailing too closely might give Frank the idea that she wanted to be spotted—which, of course, she did.

"Okay, I'm behind him now. So, he's spent the past couple of hours on these back roads?"

"That's right. He's been going over and over them, each time trying out a different turn."

"And you think he's looking for something?"

"Definitely. But what?"

Abigail shook her head. Rachel Cuthbert was currently being processed for murder, while Frank Davis prowled the outskirts of Wallace Point. If anything, he should've been making himself scarce. "James, do you think he could be looking for another victim?"

She heard him take a deep breath. "Let's hope not, Cupcake. This town has had more than enough foul play, if you ask me."

If Frank were looking for another victim, then he might as well join Rachel at the police station right then. With the two tails in tow, there was no way the guy was going to get away with another murder.

Abigail was suddenly happy she'd thrown caution to the wind to stalk Frank Davis. If she and Thor could prevent another murder simply by driving around, then she was all for it.

"I don't think he's noticed me yet," she said, her hands sweaty on the wheel.

"Good. And I take it you haven't noticed me yet either."

Abigail's heart jumped. She'd been so focused on tailing Frank, she'd forgotten that James would be tailing *her* too. She glanced into the rearview mirror. "I don't see you."

"Good."

The car ahead of Abigail turned off onto another street, leaving her right behind Frank. She eased up on the gas pedal, wanting to remain inconspicuous for as long as possible.

Beside her, Thor stared serenely out the window. Abigail had never been in this part of town, so the setting was new for both of them.

The charcoal sedan made a slow right turn onto a wooded street. Abigail followed suit. On this street there were only a few driveways, each one disappearing into a tangle of brush and trees.

The car ahead jerked to a stop, as if someone had just stomped on the brakes. Then the car continued on, driving a little faster than it had before.

"We've been spotted," Abigail said.

"It's about time. He must be very preoccupied to not have noticed you for this long. Stay on him."

"Roger."

Abigail followed Frank, not bothering to maintain a discreet distance. They made a series of turns until they were back out on the main road again. Frank's car accelerated suddenly and made a sharp left.

"He's trying to shake me."

"That's good. Stay on him a bit. Make him work to lose you."

Abigail concentrated on Frank's tail lights. The guy was driving erratically, feigning left turns when he was heading right, accelerating when he couldn't possibly gain much ground.

"I think Frank Davis is as bad at shaking a tail as I am at tailing a suspect."

"What? Nonsense, you're doing great. We've got him right where we want him. By the way, does this neighborhood seem familiar to you?"

Abigail glanced around her. She wouldn't call the area a neighborhood. The side roads Frank was taking were becoming twistier and more desolate than they had been. The trees, which had seemed friendly before, now arched high overhead, casting the street into a mid-morning twilight.

"None of this rings a bell. Why do you ask?"

"Oh, I don't know. I feel like I'm having déjà vu right now."

Abigail made another turn, only to find an empty street.

"I've lost him."

"That's okay. I think he knows where he's going now. If I lose him too, we've still got the tracker. I won't lose him though."

"You must do this a lot, James."

"I've done my share of stalking, that's for sure. Part of the PI job description, I guess. Wait, there he is. I see him."

"Where are you?"

"I'm on Carrion Way."

Abigail pulled over to the side of the road, tree branches scraping her car. Grabbing her phone, she punched the street name into the GPS.

"Abigail," James said, his voice hard. "He's stopping at a cabin. I'm pulling over to park. I'm pretty sure he hasn't seen me yet."

According to the GPS, Carrion Way was just a half mile from where she sat. She pulled the car back onto the road.

"Abigail, I know this cabin."

"What do you mean?"

"I mean I know this cabin. It's… it's where the Wallace Point Ripper took one of his victims."

"What?" She slammed on the brakes in shock. A quick glance in the rearview mirror reminded her she was lucky to be alone on the road. "What cabin?"

"The Ripper's cabin. I should have known as soon as he turned onto Carrion Way. I really should have known."

Abigail heard something in James' voice, something she'd never heard before: anxiety.

"James, wait for me. Let's call your dad."

"There isn't time, Abigail." James was breathing hard, and he didn't sound quite like himself. "I'm going in."

Before Abigail could open her mouth to protest, the call

disconnected. She dialed him immediately, but the call went straight to voicemail.

Abigail looked at Thor, her stomach a tight ball of nerves. James was in the Ripper's cabin with the man who had killed Theodore. With the memories of his mom swimming through his head, what would James do to Frank? And, now that he was backed into a corner, what would Frank do to James?

"No time to think, is there, Thor?"

Thor shifted in his seat and whimpered, sensing her anxiety.

Abigail dialed the police station. To her relief, Sheriff Wilson picked up.

"Wallace Point Sheriff's Office. Sheriff Wilson speaking."

"Sheriff Wilson, James and I have been tracking Frank Davis."

"Who is this?"

"Sorry, this is Abigail. James and I were doing some PI work and—"

"Abigail? Is your grandmother there? Let me talk to Florence."

"No, Sheriff Wilson, Grandma isn't here. It's just Abigail. I need you to listen. James put a tracker on Frank Davis's car."

"He did *what?*"

"Get angry later, Sheriff. We tailed him for a while, and now he's at the Ripper's cabin. James went in after him. I'm going in too."

"The cabin on Carrion Way?" Sheriff Wilson's voice was steady and clear.

"That's the one. I have to go, Sheriff. I have to make sure he's all right."

"Abigail, please don't—"

"There isn't time."

Abigail hung up, then switched back to her GPS. She wasn't far from the cabin. With any luck, she'd show up in time. In time for what, she wasn't sure, and she had no idea what she was going to do about it once she got there, but none of that mattered to her now.

She had to make sure James was okay.

CHAPTER TWENTY-SIX

Abigail jumped out of her car and ran up the dirt driveway, Thor right at her heels. Trees crowded around them, reaching their long, arthritic fingers to snatch at Abigail's face and clothes, but she paid no heed to them.

The cabin was old, covered in moss, and boarded up, but the front door stood ajar. The sound of raised voices reached Abigail's ears as she scrambled around the charcoal sedan and up the sagging front steps.

She burst through the front door, ready for battle. The interior of the cabin was dark, forcing Abigail to freeze. She couldn't see a thing, but she could hear plenty.

"What are you doing here?" James was yelling. Abigail had never heard him so angry, so raw. "What do you know about the Ripper?"

A woman wailed in response. "I'm sorry! I'm so sorry!"

Why was there a woman in the cabin with Frank and James? Had the guy already found another victim?

Abigail blinked, and finally her vision adjusted to the dim interior. She could see James's tall figure near the far corner of the room. At his feet, huddled on the floor, was a woman with bright red hair. It only took Abigail a moment to identify her from the home movie her mother had made: It was Monica Ives, Frank's bride to be, and possibly Theodore's lover.

"Tell me!" James snapped. "What do you know?"

Thor barked, shifting James's attention away from Monica. Abigail seized the moment. She stepped forward and put her hand gently on James's arm. "James, it's me."

James's eyes were wide and bright in the darkness. He seemed to look right through Abigail, as if she wasn't there at all. She squeezed his arm.

"James," she murmured. "It's me, Cupcake."

Finally, his eyes focused on her face. He shook his head. "Cupcake? You shouldn't be here."

Abigail glanced at the weeping woman in the corner. "You're scaring her, James. Let me try to talk to her."

James frowned, and for a moment, Abigail worried he would lose his head again. But then he shrugged and stepped back. "She was the one driving the car. Frank's nowhere to be seen."

Abigail crept toward Monica, who was crouched into a ball, her head hiding under her arms. "Monica, did Frank put you up to this?"

Monica looked up. Her face was red and splotchy, but Abigail could see the confusion in her eyes. "Frank? No, he has nothing to do with this."

"But isn't he a fan of the Ripper?" Abigail knelt so that she was eye level with Monica. "Isn't that how he knew about this cabin?"

Monica sniffled. "He used to be. That's how we met, because I was part of the fan club too." Her face crumpled and she burst into fresh tears. "God, I was so stupid. I'm sorry. I'm sorry for everything."

Abigail frowned. Why was Monica apologizing? What could she possibly have to feel sorry about in all of this?

Then, finally, the pieces of the puzzle fell into place.

"Oh," Abigail said softly. Monica Ives fell silent, though she didn't meet Abigail's eyes. Abigail took a deep breath and said, "You, Theodore, Frank, and Rachel were all part of that fan club, right? The Wallace Point Ripper brought you all together a long time ago, not just on the night of the murder."

Abigail thought about the video her mother had taken of Theodore and Monica as teens. She remembered the voice of her mother's unseen accomplice. She had thought it sounded familiar, and now she knew why. Years of smoking had altered Rachel Cuthbert's voice enough that Abigail hadn't recognized it when Rachel was younger, more innocent than she was now.

"You and Theodore were together, way back when. Eventually you moved on, but he didn't. Next thing he knows, you're all grown up and getting married, and he wasn't ready. Did he try to talk you out of the wedding? When you told him that it was over, how did he take it?"

"He threatened me." Monica spat the words as if they were bitter on her tongue. "One minute he's telling me he loves me for all eternity, the next minute he's threatening to tell Frank about an affair we never had. He was going to lie to my fiancé."

Abigail nodded. "So you turned to Rachel, your friend since high school. Between the two of you, you decided Theodore deserved to die for what he was trying to do to you."

"He was going to ruin my life," Monica murmured. "On my wedding night at that."

"And I'm sure Rachel fed that fire, didn't she? I bet she encouraged you to take care of him."

Monica nodded.

"And she figured, why not mimic the Ripper? Though you and everyone else had moved on, she was still obsessed with Wallace Point's long-lost serial killer. It gave her a chance to relive the glory days, back when exciting things happened and people actually locked their doors. Not to mention the wonders it would work for her career. And in return, you'd get to save your marriage."

Monica met Abigail's gaze. "Teddy deserved it. He wasn't just threatening my marriage. He had been stalking me for a few years now, sending me these... inappropriate messages and letters. Then he told me if he couldn't be happy, neither could I. It freaked me out. I thought he was going to do something to Frank."

"Why didn't you tell Frank what was happening?"

"Teddy said he'd use some old love letters to tell Frank 'the truth.' The creep even booked himself a room in the motel where some of my wedding guests were staying. We hadn't invited him, which I think made him angrier. I was so stressed, I didn't know what to do. So I called Rachel."

"And from there, she convinced you to take things into your own hands, didn't she? And to pin it on the Ripper?"

"She told me the Ripper would have killed Teddy. He only killed people who deserved it."

Abigail heard James shifting his weight behind her, so she hurried on. "So Rachel bought the original knife, and she told you it would be just fine. She would cover the story herself. She would suggest the Ripper was back and alarm the town. That way, no one would ever think to suspect you."

Monica looked away, not answering.

Abigail pressed further. "So you dressed in black, the way the Ripper always dressed. Told Teddy you'd meet him so you two could talk. You then took Frank's car and drove to the motel where Theodore was waiting for you. He probably thought you were coming to tell him that you finally realized you two were meant to be together, but then you stabbed him three times. Just like Rachel told you to."

Monica was absolutely still now. Tears ran down her face, but she didn't make a sound.

"Once you were sure he was dead, Rachel had you return the knife to her so she could hide it. Is that right?"

"I'm sorry," Monica whispered. "He deserved it. He really did. If he would have just let me live my life. But he couldn't do that. He was as obsessed with me as he had been with the Ripper. He didn't give me a choice."

James moved to Abigail's side and crouched down so he too was face to face with Monica. Abigail stole a quick glance at his face. He looked angry, hurt, and tired. But he looked like himself. Something in Abigail unwound and relaxed.

James began, "If it can be proven as aggravated assault, perhaps you won't spend the rest of your life in jail. But I can't say I have any sympathy for you. Dredging up a cold case, giving this town hope that the horror they've survived might finally be resolved, that's unforgivable."

"I didn't want to make it about the Wallace Point Ripper," Monica insisted. "That was Rachel's idea, and the only reason she convinced me to go along with it was because she promised it'd keep me from getting caught. She said it was the only way."

"There are always unintended consequences when people try to avoid blame. For one, you've brought back very painful memories for me and my father. By shifting the blame away from yourself, you're only shifting the hurt onto someone else."

Monica sniffled. "I'm sorry. I hadn't thought about that."

Thor was the first to hear the sirens. He barked until a

group of police cars pulled up behind Abigail's car and uniformed men jumped out. James stood up and approached the cops as Thor returned to Abigail's side. Together they watched James explain the situation to his father, who handcuffed Monica while shaking his head.

Sheriff Wilson's face was a mask of incredulity. The case had obviously had too many twists and turns for his liking. Abigail was just happy the sheriff had pulled himself together when she'd needed him.

After Sheriff Wilson took their statements, he told them they were free to go. "And Abigail." He paused by the door of the unkempt cabin. "Thanks for keeping an eye on my boy."

James rolled his eyes as he turned toward Abigail. The tension from the past month seemed to be melting right off his face. "This whole chase has made me hungry. Think your grandma's baked up some fresh cookies for our triumphant return?"

"Probably not. She has no idea we just caught a murderer." Abigail paused. "What's up with everybody and Grandma's cookies, anyway?"

James shrugged. "What can I say?"

For a moment, Abigail hesitated. Then she took a deep breath and spoke in a low voice. "I feel like after what we just went through, I can share a very dark secret with you. It's been eating at me ever since I moved here."

The look on James's face turned to one of concern. He stooped so that he was closer to Abigail's height and whispered, "What is it?"

Abigail looked around to make sure no one else was within earshot. "Grandma's cookies are from a container," she confessed. "Like, straight out of the refrigerated section of the grocery store."

James regarded Abigail very seriously. He looked around and then whispered, "I know. The whole town knows. But we'll never admit it because we all adore her, and it gives us an excuse to stop by every day." He patted Abigail's shoulder as a sly smile formed on his face. "Now you have to keep an even darker secret."

Abigail stepped back, stunned. And here she had thought the mess at the cabin was the most shocking revelation of the day.

CHAPTER TWENTY-SEVEN

Sunlight streamed in through the front windows at Whodunit Antiques. From the warmth and comfort of the store, the day looked bright and happy. As Abigail had discovered on her morning run, however, the sun did nothing to ease the biting cold wind.

Grandma stood with Piper Fischer before a floor length mirror. The two were whispering and giggling in hushed tones.

Abigail stood at the checkout counter, watching Missy. "She's telling someone else, isn't she girl?"

Missy sat at her feet, peering around the counter and in the direction of the whispers.

"Don't worry, Missy. You just keep running with Thor and me, and we'll have your girlish figure back in no time."

The front door swung open and James walked in, his

trench coat flapping in the frigid draft that followed him. "Good morning, ladies."

"James!" Grandma cooed. "How wonderful to see you again."

"Hey, Granny Lane. Did you miss me already? It's only been a couple of days."

"We haven't all been busy putting criminals behind bars," said Piper. "Our days are just a little less exciting than yours."

"Nonsense. Abigail here puts criminals behind bars *and* finds the time to help out at the store." James grinned at Abigail.

Piper sighed. "I still can't believe you two went on a high-speed car chase."

Abigail frowned. "We didn't—"

"They didn't think a thing of it," Grandma interrupted. "These youngsters will dive into any situation as long as it's dangerous and exciting. They make me feel quite old. In fact, I think I need to get off my feet for a bit."

"Oh, I'll let you get your rest, Granny Lane." Piper turned toward Abigail and James. "Next time you two go on another adventure, call me!" With a wave, Piper floated out of the front door and into the cold morning.

Grandma made her way back to the counter and straightened up, no longer looking quite tired. "So, James, what's new?"

"Well, both Monica Ives and Rachel Cuthbert have officially been arrested for the murder of Theodore Howard. The case is closed."

Grandma smiled as she settled into a nearby armchair. "That's not news. Give me something my friends don't already know."

"All right, how's this for gossip? Frank isn't breaking his engagement to Monica."

"That's more like it," Grandma said. "Is he aware she killed a man?"

"Yes, ma'am. He knows every sordid detail. Of course, he doesn't support the whole murder part of it. But he says he understands that Theodore pushed Monica into a corner. He knows that Monica has been true to him, regardless of Teddy's meddling, and that's enough for Frank Davis."

Now that Abigail was certain Frank was innocent, she felt pretty sorry for the guy. After all, his fiancée had called off their wedding and completely upended his whole life. And if that weren't bad enough, she was now in jail for murdering an old boyfriend. Talk about a bad break.

"If only she had simply been honest with Frank," Abigail mused. "He seems pretty devoted to her."

James nodded. "Yeah, he actually brought that up. He told Monica he wouldn't have let Theodore's claims change his mind about marrying her."

"If anything, the true criminal in all of this is that Rachel Cuthbert," Grandma said. "Who encourages a friend to murder another person?"

Abigail answered, "Someone who cares more about her career than the people in her life. She had a man killed, put this whole town in a panic, all for the pleasure of seeing her name in the paper again. It's bewildering how someone can be that selfish."

"The judge and jury definitely won't go easy on her," James said. "Speaking of Rachel, I'm actually going to see her this afternoon."

Grandma's eyes grew wide. "You are? To be honest, James, I'm surprised. Are you sure you want to?"

"I think I need to. I talked it over with Dad and we both think this might be a way to get some closure." He looked over at Abigail. "What do you say, Cupcake?"

"You want me to come with you?"

James shrugged. "It might be nice to have a friend with me."

Abigail glanced at Grandma, who gave her the slightest of nods.

"Fine," Abigail agreed. "But you owe me for all the work I've missed chasing you around."

"Do you accept ice cream as a form of payment?" James asked with a grin.

"As long as it's not strawberry flavored."

James clutched his chest. "Oh, my heart! How can you malign the best ice cream flavor humanity has ever known?"

Abigail waved him off and followed him outside. At least he seemed to be feeling better.

THAT AFTERNOON, the station was all but deserted when

Abigail and James walked in. Sheriff Wilson awaited them, his face a mix of concern and relief.

"The officers have been working long hours the past month," he explained when he caught Abigail's eyes wandering around the empty building. "Most of them are catching up on some much-needed time off. They're not here to say it, but they have you to thank for that."

Abigail couldn't help but smile. She hadn't thought much about the officers who'd been working the case, but she could see how it would have kept them away from their homes and families.

Sheriff Wilson led them to the back of the station, where a handful of jail cells lined a single hallway. The cells were vacant except for one.

Rachel lay on her cot with her feet propped up on the wall. When Abigail and James came into view, she eyed them upside down before lazily sitting up.

"Well, if it isn't my two detective friends." Her voice was gravelly and she had dark circles under her brown eyes. "Come to gloat?"

"We came to talk," James said. He grabbed a couple of folding chairs and set them up in front of the jail cell. "We're hoping to get the full story, Rachel," he said as he sat down. "I'm still confused about a few things."

Rachel watched as Abigail lowered herself into her chair, paying James no heed. "I'm sure if I had a lawyer, he'd tell me to remain silent."

"He probably would. Why don't you have one?"

"I know I'm not getting out of this mess. Might as well begin my penance now, rather than delaying it."

James hesitated before saying, "That's not advisable, denying your right to a lawyer."

"Whatever. What do you want to know?"

"Where did you go when you disappeared?" Abigail asked, the first question on her mind.

"I was at the Ripper's cabin, burying the knife. I figured eventually the cops would think to look there, and once they found it, that'd make them certain that the Ripper did it."

"Why were you gone for so long, though?"

Rachel shrugged. "I don't know. There was a lot of heat on me, with the newspaper putting me on probation, and *James* here asking me a million questions anytime he saw me. So I decided to take a few days off from Wallace Point, before my nerves got the best of me."

James shifted in his seat. "Why did you end up digging up the knife again, if you had hidden it?"

"Monica called me up, after Frank had been taken in for questioning. She told me we had to confess. I told her Frank would be fine. He didn't do it after all, so he'd eventually get released, but there was no convincing her. She said she wasn't going to let Frank take the fall; either one or both of us were going down for what happened."

Rachel sighed, her hand reaching up to her mouth for a cigarette that wasn't there. "That was about when I realized things had spun pretty far out of our control. We never meant to involve Frank. And, for what it's worth, I'm sorry for the pain this brought back for you and your dad. When I hatched up this plan, I didn't really consider the trauma it would unearth."

"Didn't you?" Abigail asked. "Because it really seems like you were banking on that emotional reaction."

Rachel shot Abigail a dark look. "I confessed, didn't I?"

James spoke up. "After you confessed, why did Monica go out looking for the cabin?"

"She wanted to burn it down." Rachel half-smiled. "She told me that, last night. We were cell neighbors before they took her to who knows where. I had no idea about that 'high-speed chase' until she told me. That gave me a kick. A high-speed chase between a sedan and a VW Bug? She always was so melodramatic."

"Why did she want to burn the cabin down?" James pressed.

"That cabin was kind of a shrine for the club. We used to meet there and do these little rituals and leave offerings for the Ripper. We even held a couple of séances, in case the Ripper had died and wanted to reach out to us. He never did. Monica was ashamed of all that. She wanted to destroy everything the Ripper had left behind. I guess she was just as riddled with guilt as I was." Rachel paused, looking up. "Did she do it? Burn the cabin down? She didn't get around to telling me."

Abigail shook her head. "James caught up with her just as she was going inside the cabin. Seems like she couldn't remember where it was, so we found her before she found it."

Rachel looked away. "Maybe that's a good thing. That cabin is part of Wallace Point's history."

On that note, James stood. He folded his chair and faced Rachel. "I'm glad this whole ordeal is over."

Rachel laughed, a short, harsh bark of a laugh. "It's over for you. It's just beginning for me."

"Serves you right."

Outside, Abigail and James drew in deep breaths of fresh air. The cold actually felt good on her cheeks. It reminded her that she was alive and free.

"Well, that definitely wasn't the closure I was hoping for," James finally said.

Abigail laughed. "I know what you mean. I can't tell if she actually feels sorry about killing a guy, or if she's just sorry she got caught."

"I wonder if it's a little bit of both? Anyhow, what are you doing tonight, Cupcake?"

"I was planning on grabbing a cozy blanket, sitting by the fire while I read a—" Abigail stopped. Her eyes narrowed. "Actually, Grandma had suggested that I do that. She knows it's my 'catnip,' as she called it."

James had a blank look on his face. "Catnip?"

Abigail sighed. "Yeah, it's how she controls people. Grandma wants some girl time, I think. But I'm free tomorrow night. Have you dug up another case?"

"Not in the least. I was thinking of going to Kirby's Candlepin Alley for a game and a celebratory drink."

Abigail watched the quiet street before them. School was just letting out, and little bundles of sweaters and boots were making their way down the sidewalk.

Grabbing a drink with James would sound a lot like a date to Grandma. Was she willing to endure her grandmother's knowing glances and coy smiles? Abigail sighed. The case was closed and James would be moving back to New Jersey soon. The least she could do was bowl a game or two with the guy.

Besides, celebrating the end of the case sounded like fun. She was proud she had helped solve the case, but, more than that, she was happy that it was all behind them.

"A game sounds good," she said at last. "Tomorrow, then."

CHAPTER TWENTY-EIGHT

The next morning, Abigail had no desire to run. Thor rolled his massive torso onto her face. She pushed him off. Then another smaller torso rolled onto her face. Abigail sat up hard, and Missy went tumbling over the side of the bed.

"Oh, jeez, Missy, I'm so sorry!" Abigail reached over, plucked up the cream and white puff ball, and deposited the dog onto her lap. "Why aren't you with Grandma?"

Missy scampered to the foot of the bed and returned with her leash in her mouth.

"Missy, you've got to be kidding. You're slimmer than ever. And it's cold out! Are you sure you want to run?"

Missy simply sat, waiting.

"Oh, all right then," Abigail gave in. Thor, absolutely

delighted, leaped beside Missy and sent her tumbling off the bed again.

WHEN THEY RETURNED from their jog, Sheriff Wilson's patrol car was parked outside the antique store.

"Looks like Grandma's got her beau back," Abigail commented to the two dogs, who sniffed the tires before continuing up the front porch.

Grandma and Sheriff Wilson were in the kitchen, chatting over a cup of tea.

"Good morning, Abigail," Grandma called. "How was the run?"

"Not bad. Missy and I are improving at about the same rate."

Grandma shook her head. "I don't know what's gotten into my little princess." She patted her knees, and Missy jumped up into her lap. "She's turning into quite the athlete."

"Maybe she's trying to get Thor's attention." Abigail smiled and turned to Sheriff Wilson. "How are you, Sheriff?"

"I'm better than I was," Willy responded. After a quick appraising glance, Abigail decided he really was doing better. His shoulders had lost their stoop, and his eyes were clearer, his face less pale.

"I'm glad this case is over," he continued. "And I'm glad it's only tangentially related to the Ripper. I'm ready to move on with my life."

Grandma nodded. "I think we all are."

"I'm not so sure about James, though," he admitted. "I'm worried he'll never put things in the past. He just can't rest until a question's answered. He's a lot like his mother in that way."

Sheriff Wilson's voice cracked. Abigail wasn't sure what to do, but Grandma did. She reached out a wrinkled hand and placed it over the sheriff's. She didn't speak; she just gave him the time to feel his grief, his loss, and then put himself together again, as he had every day since his wife's death.

After a while, he spoke again. "I'm just happy James is staying in town for a while. I missed that boy."

Abigail tilted her head. "He is?"

The sheriff nodded, a smile taking over his face. "He told me he wants to help out for a bit. Keep me company. He's always been a good kid."

Abigail glanced over at Grandma, who winked back at her. The old woman was relentless with her attempts at playing matchmaker. Abigail would have to make sure she knew nothing about where she was going tonight, and with whom, because then she'd never hear the end of it.

CHAPTER TWENTY-NINE

Kirby's Candlepin Bowling Alley was just as crowded as the night Abigail had met and questioned Rachel. When Abigail joined James at the bar, he nodded at the busy lanes. "Guess we're not bowling after all, Cupcake."

She sat on the empty stool next to him and looked around. Families and couples clustered around the lanes, while teens stuck to arcade games along the sides of the large open room.

"Everything seems so normal," she said, yelling to make herself heard over the noise.

James followed her gaze around the room. After a moment, he smiled. "Yeah. Good old Wallace Point."

"Abigail," barked a gruff voice. Abigail looked up. Behind the bar, Kirby towered over her. He looked pretty angry.

"Hey Kirby," she said. "Busy night."

Kirby glanced up, his face growing darker. "More people out, now that the killer has been caught. Thanks a lot."

Was he really thanking her, or was he being sarcastic? He certainly didn't seem happy about the influx of customers. Abigail sighed. Kirby was one of those mysteries she might never solve. "Um, you're welcome. Business has picked up for Grandma too."

Kirby's frown softened. "Good. I'm glad she's well."

James nudged Abigail's shoulder. "So, Cupcake, what are you drinking?"

A COUPLE of hours and a few drinks later, the bowling alley had quieted down enough for James and Abigail to have an actual conversation.

"I still can't believe you suspected I might have taken out Rachel," James said, doing his best to hold back his laughter.

Abigail wiped away a tear. "Of course I suspected you. You seemed like a sleazy divorce PI. Still do, if I'm going to be honest."

"Well, the job *is* necessarily sleazy at times. Divorces and cheaters are my bread and butter. Without them, I wouldn't get to wear this trench coat or use that awesome monocular Granny Lane gave me."

"Have you used it already?"

"Every day."

"What? How?"

"You'd be surprised how handy one of those things can be in daily life. Anyways, the sleazy stuff keeps me in business, but I prefer more complicated cases, the ones police have given up on. You know, missing persons, cold cases, so on and so forth."

Abigail nodded. Briefly, she wondered whether James could help her find her father. Her mother had stayed pretty tight-lipped about him, but maybe James could dig something up...

"Unfortunately, those cases don't pay much, if anything," James continued. "I investigate most of them pro bono."

"Wow. That's generous."

"I guess. I don't know. The people involved in those cases have suffered so much already. They've waited for years to find out what happened to their loved ones. I know what that feels like." James stared down into his beer. "Funny thing is, even though I've helped close a few cold cases for other people, I still can't close the Ripper case."

Abigail tried to think of something positive to say. "Well. You know. They've been closing all kinds of unsolved cases these days, with DNA forensics and databases."

"That's like playing the lottery." James shook his head. "It's up to chance if a relative of the killer decides to sequence their DNA. Even then, the police have to realize it's a match. I don't think my man's going to be caught that way."

Abigail finished her drink, and, before she could say a word, Kirby refilled it. She chuckled. Maybe he drank like a Viking, and thought she could too.

"So, what do you plan on doing now?" she asked, taking a tiny sip. "Your father said that you're going to be staying for a while?"

"That's right. My father's been under a lot of stress lately, so I want to help out any way I can." James paused and gave Abigail a cryptic look. "I don't want anyone to catch on, especially not my father, but I'm going to give the Ripper case a second look. It was such a turbulent time in this town back when it happened that I wouldn't be surprised if the police missed a crucial detail."

Abigail didn't know what to say to that. The fact that he wanted to continue hunting the Ripper worried her. Chasing the killer might simply be an exercise in futility. James had lived most of his life in the shadow of the Ripper's murders. If he wasn't careful, he risked squandering the rest of his days in an endless search for a killer who might've already been dead or, even worse, had put the past behind him.

Still, if James wanted to keep searching for the Ripper, that was entirely his prerogative.

"I hope you do find something new," she said. "You know who to call if you need any help."

"Thanks, Cupcake."

"So, where are you staying in the meanwhile? Your father's place?"

"Actually, I'm staying at the murder motel."

Abigail's mouth dropped open. "Why?"

"It's a blank slate. Wouldn't want to distract myself with the nostalgia of my childhood home. That and I get a kick out of the motel owner, Mary Chang. Can you believe she yelled at me for never making my bed?" James grinned. "Like, come on, I was busy trying to solve a murder that happened in *her* motel. Not to mention I thought bed making was what room service was for!"

Abigail laughed. She could totally picture Mary Chang getting on James's case.

Just then, the lights in the bowling alley dimmed perceptibly: Kirby's signal that he was ready to close up for the evening.

"Come on, Cupcake. I'll walk you home." James drained his drink and stood. Abigail eyed her own beverage before pushing it away. Looking around the alley one last time, Abigail smiled. Good old Wallace Point.

ABOUT THE AUTHOR

Mysteries run in the family, starting all the way back to my great grandmother. I grew up watching old black and white movies like The Thin Man and Rebecca, and reading classic mysteries by Poe, Doyle, and Christie.

Outside of writing mysteries, I love old steamships, 1990s adventure puzzle games, and trusty pets. I live in a coastal New England town with my hideous (yet charming) Chihuahua, Fugly.

Made in the USA
San Bernardino, CA
20 June 2019